Cafe Days

Cafe
Days

George Bothamley

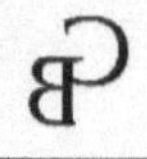

For lovers, losers and loners

Create Art For Eternity

Don't Abandon Your Soul

When I lost my job, I was close to losing my mind too; and found myself in a situation where I had only four options available for me.

The first, was to try and make it back to my home country – though I could not afford the flight, or the boat, or the train, or even a damn bus ride at that point! (And, having come to this country illegally anyway . . . there was no chance of being smuggled back the way I came in.)

The second option, was pretty much to try my luck out on the streets – and see how long it took to get killed, because I didn't own anything valuable enough to get robbed.

The third, was just to give up on this life entirely. Something I am ashamed to have even considered now.

And the fourth option – the one I eventually settled on – was to take a cleaning job in a dirty little café; located in one of the roughest areas of the inner city.

At the time, it felt like the single worst period of my life.

I was entirely alone – with only the most basic English language skills.

I was too shy – and too traumatised – and too self-conscious about my accent, to feel able to make any genuine connections.

And, on the city's part too – we all know how everything has a habit of just moving so quickly here; making it too easy to feel as if the world is just passing you by.

But you know – time is a funny thing.

And when I look back on it all now, there is something about those days which also feel somehow golden for me.

Yes, I was lonely as hell. But I also came to realise how this loneliness of mine gave me the unique opportunity of observing the city in its most raw form. Not from high up above, as I had been in my previous job as a tall building window cleaner . . . but, literally, from ground level.

Down in the dirt.

Where everything is that much more real.

And, essentially, this is why I began writing these little passages of mine too; using notebooks, scrap pieces of paper, napkins, or whatever else I had immediately to hand at the time.

At first it was my only way of expressing, because I had no-one else to talk to.

But, in time, as my English language skills improved – this writing became a way for me to feel as if I was partaking in this world again. Even if it was only as an observer.

I was recording these little episodes of life happening around me each day – from the very best, to the very worst, that our society can offer. And, at the same time, I found myself exploring my own mind too; facing up to certain things which I was sure I had buried.

So, I guess you could say that in the worst days of my life, I found the best possible escape. And though so much time has passed now – and the actual Café I worked in has long since been closed – I have been using my most recent period of unemployment to sort through all of the pieces of writing I kept from that time.

To be honest, they have been making such a mess scattered all around my home for all these years – it was long overdue that I should do something about them!

And, essentially, I had two choices.

Either throw them all on a bonfire.

Or put them all in a book!

I hope I made the right decision.

Vinny

The rock and the hard place

At one end of this street, there is a church
dedicated to St Jude; the patron saint of lost causes
and hopeless cases.

At the other end of this street, there is a whorehouse; where,
as far as I've heard, the women can either take you to heaven
or send you to hell – depending on what you're in to.

And, all the way around this neighbourhood; you go from
squatters digs, drug spots, late night bars and dirty arcades –
to pawn shops, boarded up windows, taxi offices, and
bookmakers.
Kind of like you're travelling on the direct line between a
rock and a hard place.

But, right here in the centre of the street, is a
funny little place.

Tired
Neglected
Dirty as hell
But trying to be clean.

The Silver Spoon Café.

A place of stories

There's a tubby fella sitting in the corner over there who hasn't stopped looking at his phone for the last half an hour.

Literally, he's eating a sandwich with one hand.
He opened his packet of crisps with one hand.
He poured himself a cup of coffee with one hand.
And, a little while ago, I saw him come out the men's room too – still, with his eyes glued to that screen of his.

So, lord knows what managed to do in there with one hand!
But I can only hope he at least washed up afterwards too – even if it was only one handed!
Or maybe he'll get around to that later on, if he ever puts the damn phone down!

Then, a few tables across from him, you've got three ladies. All with the same hairstyle . . . just in different colours.

For them, the last half an hour has been spent psychoanalysing one of the senior managers in their office. And, you wouldn't believe just how much they have to say about it all.

"She's so judgemental"

"Yeah, I know! So two-faced."

"Did you see the way she was flirting with Terry yesterday?"

"I don't know. All I've heard is her moaning so far"

"She's always bitching about someone "

*"And did you hear the way she was speaking to me yesterday too . . .
as if I was her little pet"*

"No respect at all"
"Who does she think she is!"

"I know"
"Just rise above it"

"She's probably just jealous."
"Wishes she was young again"

"That's why she looks down her nose at everyone"

"Yeah. Such a snob"

"So judgemental"

Honestly, they went on like this for so long . . . I had to go
for a break. I've never felt so stressed out by a manager that
I've never even met!

But, by the time I came back around to cleaning the tables close to them again, the three of them had finally moved on to a new topic.

This time, the new young intern. Who, apparently, had committed the sin of turning down the chance to share lunch with them today.

"Yeah, I'm glad she didn't join us anyway.
Don't you think she seems a little weird?"

"Oh, I know . . . something's definitely not right there."

"And did you see that suit she was wearing today?
"Horrendous!"

"That low cut top . . . does she really think she can pull that off?"

"Her parents probably haven't given her enough pocket money to afford something that actually fits yet!"

"And did you see when she dropped all those books on the floor?"

"Good God . . . if she can't even carry a few books, how will she ever cope on a real assignment!"

"I think she only got the job because Paul fancies her"

"Needs to go back to school, if you ask me. She's not ready for the real world yet"

And here, the group of them started cackling together.
As I just walked away again, thinking;
"Wow. Are you sure it's the senior manager and the new intern who are the real problems here!"

Then . . .

What else is happening in here today?

Man, the whole place is full of stories, really!

You've got a young mother over there with two kids – desperately trying to make the smaller one eat something while, simultaneously, trying to stop the bigger one from eating absolutely everything.

You've got a skinny guy standing by the drinks fridge . . . agonising for god only knows how long over whether he should get the orange juice or the apple juice.

You've got Big Bob sitting on one of the armchairs. Just finished his second bacon sandwich, and now making his steady way through a plate of chips that is supposed to feed a family.

You've got Klara the waitress behind the counter, having a flirt with some idiot in a parka jacket – even though, for the

entire day up until this point, she's been scowling at just
about every person she sees, and has barely said a word to
anyone else except for a curt "yes" and "there you go"

And, finally, over here;
sitting in the little window seat
you've got *me*.

Just sipping on day old coffee,
because it's the only thing available for me.

And talking to a piece of paper –
for much the same reason.

The Pen and the Page

I've never been much good at conversation.

But at one point or another,
everybody needs someone
to talk to!

And when a man is lonely enough for long enough;
he makes mighty good friends with the pen and the page!

Stains

I've been working in this place for the best part of three years at this point. But, rest assured, I know it still doesn't look like much.

No matter how hard I scrub the walls . . . they're still yellowing.
No matter how many times I mop the floors . . . there are still stains that won't lift.
And no matter how many times I wipe the windows . . . they'll still be half cracked.

Plus, most of the lamplights in here are broken.

The bins rarely get collected on time.

The radio seems to only show up for work every so often – much like a lot of the other staff too!

And we stopped serving food in here around 6 months ago, because it turned out our last chef was robbing the place!

So, suffice to say, The Silver Spoon Café is not exactly the finest establishment in the city!

But, still – I bet it could be a hell of a lot nicer than it is, if we all just tried a little harder.

I mean, this might be the number one spot for Lowlifes, Good Time Charlies, Drunks, Villains, Weirdos, Workers, and Wasters. . .

But, that still doesn't mean it has to be a goddam mess all the time!

Caring

I don't care for the modern world
And the modern world takes care of me

And I care for the modern people
And the modern people don't care for me

See yourself in everything

If you look at this world for long enough,
you'll see yourself in everything.

For example, this afternoon, when I was sweeping up outside, I saw a guy sitting on a roof terrace with all his buddies.

No doubt, this guy was having a real good day, at the end of a real good week – which is why he had assembled a few fair-weather friends to help him celebrate.

 And, when he raised his glass to make a toast, I bet he was drinking to *"more life"*
The kind of thing that someone would only say if they're yet to fully understand what "more life" can even do to a man!

But when he goes home later . . . I wonder if he feels something else too.

I wonder if he ever sits on his own, like I do; to find all those old insecurities running all along the windowsill again.

Or, I wonder if doubts and regrets come tapping at his door just a little too often. . . Constantly making him wonder if this *"more life"* thing really is worth it after all!

Ahh . . . who knows.
I guess every man thinks his own thoughts.

But you know, it's not just him.
I have this bad habit of seeing myself in just about everyone
these days.

Like this young kid here, just stepping into the café,
desperately clinging on to his father's hand.

Clearly, he's terrified of absolutely every single thing in this
world, and just wants to go back home again.
And, honestly – who can blame him!

When you reach that age where you are just old enough to
start realising how much of a struggle this living can be,
it's no surprise he's looking for a reassuring hand to hold.
(I'm still looking for one too . . . and I must be three times
this kid's age!)

And then
just across the street from here,
you've got another young fella.

This one, maybe in his mid-twenties
sitting on a bench all alone.

He doesn't seem to be a tramp or a down and out;
his shoes are a bit too shiny for that.

In fact, he's dressed immaculately.
Like he might have had somewhere really special he was
supposed to be today.

But, still
you can just tell he must be down on his luck in some way.

He's been sitting there on his own since morning.
Just staring vacantly at the floor,
and watching the traffic passing him by
while wiping a tear from his eyes every so often.

Ahh . . . it's tough, my man!

I know that bench well.

Reality

Sad to say,
but reality doesn't care about feelings.

The sun doesn't shine brighter in order to make us happy.

The rains and the storms will rage, no matter if it's good or
bad for us

The darkness will come – whether you fear it or not.

The city – and the world – will just keep moving.
No matter what happens to anybody.

And when you believe you've finally lost everything –
Give it some time.

Soon enough, you'll see that you can always
lose a little more.

Two of every creature

The Silver Spoon Café is like the entire city (or maybe even
the entire world) condensed into one little microcosm.

Call it a sample of a sick society.

A modern-day Noah's ark . . .

Only, instead of two of every kind of creature,
We get two of every lover,
loser,
loner,
liar . . .
And about ten of every kind of lonely soul –
all just trying to find somewhere to be!

Yeah, that's all most of us want, isn't it!

No matter where it is
Or what it looks like

Everyone needs somewhere to be!

Sat here watching strangers

Every once in a while, when I'm sat here watching strangers I fall in love – to the point that I'm over here genuinely thinking about marrying someone who's name I'll never even get to know.

Crazy – isn't it!

Ninety percent of my life – I feel like I'm cold as a motherfucking stone.
And yet, the moment you show me a pretty face – I'll be falling all over myself for real.

I'll look at those eyes
Or I'll see that smile
Or I'll watch that walk.

And then . . . all of a sudden,
I'll stop

Just thinking

"Wait . . .

Don't I know you?"

"Oh, yeah . . .

Definitely!

Didn't I fall in love with you once before?

Around this time last year, maybe?

Or
If it wasn't you . . .
Then, at least,
it was someone like you; right?

Yeah!!

That's it!!

It wasn't you.

It was just someone like you.

In a place like this.

On a day like today.

At around this time in the afternoon too,
if I'm not mistaken.

Wow.

I'd forgotten all about that!"

And by now – whoever I just fell in love with, is probably
already half way out the door again,

Walking off into the world, never knowing that I even
existed –
as I just stand here and smile to myself;
thinking

"Well . . .

See you next year, I guess!"

The difficult client

Sitting across the way today, I overheard one of the hookers from down the road talking to her friend about a particular regular she was having trouble with.

Apparently, this guy had been making her feel real self-conscious; because, though he'd been coming to see her once a month for the best part of a year now – he'd spend their entire hour together just wanting to talk.

"Literally" the woman said *"it's the weirdest thing.*
Because he's not a bad looking guy. And I'm pretty sure he's loaded too. But all he ever does is just sit there blushing – asking me how my day's been, or if I've seen any good movies recently

And at first, I was like "Ok. Maybe he's a virgin or just too shy to initiate" . . . *because, obviously, we've all been there with first timers. But, a couple of times now, I've even tried to make the move with him myself. Sitting right there on his skinny ass lap.*
And, still, all he does is squirm away again,
Saying something like
"No! Stop. Wait. Let's not do that yet. I mean . . . maybe later."
Then, it's right back to.
"First, just tell me – how's your day? What've you been up to? Have you got any plans for the summer? Hasn't the weather been warm today?"

And here, the woman's friend just shook her head

"Wow. That's . . . bizarre. And he still pays full price?"

"With a tip too!

"Is he married?
Gay?
Religious?
What's his deal?"

"Who knows!
All he's told me is that he moved to this area about a year ago . . . but
is still struggling to meet new people, and doesn't really have any friends.
So, I really can't get my head around it.
He's either the creepiest guy in the city – or the loneliest. But whatever
it is, I think I'm gonna have to ghost him soon.
I'm not trying to catch a clingy here"

Then, her friend nodded

"Yeah. that's what I would do. Just block his number and
let him get on with it. You can't be too careful with creeps
like that"

And here, I couldn't help feeling kind of sorry for the poor
guy; wondering how he's gonna feel in a few weeks' time –
when he realises that the closest thing he has to a friend is
no longer returning his calls!

I mean, sure; it's not my place to judge really.

These girls can handle their business a hell of a lot better than I ever could – so, if the guy really is a psycho; then that's a whole other story.

But still, it seems far more likely that the poor fella is just feeling lost;
out here on his own in a new city . . . lacking any intelligent conversation during the day . . . going to dinner alone each night . . . trying to resist the temptation to drink, sniff, or shoot his heartache away.

And, like any one of us, all he wants is a little bit of company for a while. Someone to come home to – even if he has to pay for the damn privilege!

Yeah, it's weird;
there's no doubt about that.

But at the end of the day, if he's just wanting to talk . . .
would it really be so hard to listen?

And, either way, is he really any different from all the drunks or drug fellas who come in here late at nights too?
The guys who are also spending money they don't have, on whatever shit they're into . . .
just hoping that it'll stop them from feeling so alone.

We all have different coping strategies, I guess.

Restless

When things are quiet in here,
it's too easy to start feeling restless.

Like today. I'll be over there cleaning the front windows
and thinking;

"Look – there's a whole world out there, Vinny.
What the hell are you doing in a dirty city like this?

After everything you've been through too!
And everything you've lost. . .

You're lonelier than the creepy guy those hookers were talking about .
. . only, at least he has the money to actually pay for someone's company
Whereas, you?
You barely have enough to pay someone a damn compliment!

So – what are you staying for?
Just leave.
Run away.
Live in a van.
Escape to the forest.
Join the French foreign legion.
Anything!

Just do something different"

Or – better yet.

I'll be wiping the mirrors instead

And when I'm looking at my own tired reflection – I'm thinking.

'Lord, what the hell happened here?
Who's this idiot, standing where I'm supposed to be?

Why does he look like he hasn't eaten in a damn month?

Why are his eyes so dark!

I mean, for god's sake
This isn't the way things were supposed to be!

And is this really how I'm supposed to carry on too?

Man, I can't be having that!

Something's got to change.

Give me another chance . . .
I'd change these clothes
and this hair
and this face
and this body
and this mind
and this heart

Everything!

Seriously
Just let me change every single thing!
Because I'd really rather be someone else by now!"

But . . . soon enough,
the mirror is as clean as I can make it.

And when the next job comes – or it starts to get a little
busier in here, with more people to watch – all this shit in
my head tends to die down again.

I escape into the lives – and the messes – and the dirt – of
others;
And in doing so; I am set free!

Or, at least,
I am able to live a lie for a while.

Everyone knows

Police paid us a little visit in here today.

Apparently, two nights ago, a young fella got killed in the alleyway just down the street.
So, the boys in blue came to ask if they could have a look at our security cameras (which haven't worked for about 5 years!) – or to see if anyone had noticed anything suspicious.

But, of course, nobody knows a thing.

We've got a full house of our daytime regulars in here this afternoon – taxi drivers, labour workers, tramps, old men, street girls – and, of course . . . not a single one of them knows a damn thing!

But, it's strange, isn't it?

Because, a little while ago – before the police arrived – when many of these exact same people were first in here . . . absolutely all of them were talking about what had happened.

They knew the name of the guy who got killed –
and which gang he was affiliated with –
and what drugs he used to sell –
and why a couple of other rival dealers might have been after him, for usurping their spot –

and which club he'd last been seen at that night, where he'd apparently had a little altercation with some punk in a grey baseball cap.

They knew where the victim bought a bag of chips as he headed back this way—
and what time he'd been seen walking into the alley—
and how many shots had been fired –
and how a dark blue car with blacked out windows had pulled up a little while later . . . picking up two young fellas from the street side – one of whom was wearing a grey baseball cap.

And, on top of knowing all of that – everyone in here also knew that these two killers were never going to get away with what they'd done.

They knew that the victim's buddies were some of the *"hardest bastards in the entire city"* – and, as a unit, were already planning on hunting down this son of a bitch in the grey cap.

So, it's just weird – that's all!
How it seems like this life isn't so much about what you know . . . or who you know . . . but, rather, *who you tell it too*!

And no doubt, in a month or two's time, it will all happen again.

There will be another body

in another alleyway
in another neighbourhood,
not too far away from here.

And when it's discovered –
Absolutely everyone will be talking about it like it was all so
damn inevitable.

But of course; these conversations will only be in certain
circles – right?

Because when the police go making their enquiries for that
one too . . . you can guarantee that, once again, no-one will
know a thing about it.

Talking to myself

Ah, if only I'd been here that night.

If only I'd heard the shots.

Or seen this car.

Or caught a glimpse of this grey cap guy.

If only I had been out on park and street duty.

Then . . .

Then what, Vinny?

You really think you'd have been the one to go ahead and share it with the police?

Boy – don't be ridiculous.

You know you're too much of a coward for something like that.

That's why you're a cleaner. Not a damn vigilante!

So, just stay in your lane, will you!

Enough of all this angst.

You really want to help out in this situation?

Then go wash away some of the blood stains in that alley.

Or go see the flowers that the victim's mother has put there
for him . . .
and tell her you'll take care of them,
and make sure those petals look as fresh as they can, for as
long as possible.

That's all you can do.

Community

You'd think that in a city as big as this, with all these people everywhere – no-one would ever feel alone.

But then again, in a city as rich as this too – with all this money exchanging hands – you'd think just about everyone would be looked after, or fed, or have a place to call home. And we all know that's not the case!

So, sadly, a city like this will always be the same; with an abundance of everything but a fair share of nothing.

Split

The surface is never the full story.

When looked at from afar, this city is all bright lights and
sparkling windows.
But when seen from ground level . . . it's all dirty streets and
polluted air.

And, clearly, it's a similar story with the people here too.

You've got everyone claiming that this is a city of endless
opportunities; where all dreams come true.

And yet, in a neighbourhood like this – you realise just how
many dreams are dying out here too. And just how limited
opportunities can be!

So, it's like we're trapped in this same old cycle.

Where a small percentage are doing well –
and larger percentage are doing badly –
and, the vast majority of people
are just somewhere in between;

Pretending they're doing well;
when, all the while
behind the scenes,
things are really starting to fall apart.

Didn't we used to
build cathedrals?

Guy in the café tells me that a new skyscraper just got
commissioned a few blocks away from here.

Apparently, it's going to be 700 metres high,
made of solid glass,
and shooting straight upwards,
like a colossal middle finger to the whole damn city

Imagine that!

No doubt
it'll have all the modern features.
with reflective windows
and silver rooftop
and laser light shows at night,
which will help in blocking out just a little bit more of that
pesky starlight.

Oh . . . and who do you think will populate this new wonder
of the world?

Are they building it as a hospital?
Or a school?
Or a homeless shelter?

No – probably not.

Chances are, the top floors will be reserved as a fancy hotel.

And the rest of it will just be rented out to whoever bids the most;
with investment bankers
estate agents
accountancy firms
multi-national companies . . .
maybe a restaurant or cocktail bar here and there too, if we're lucky!

Man . . . what happened to this city?

Didn't we used to build cathedrals?

Imagine

Can you imagine being given birdsong
and drowning it out with the sound of engines?

Can you imagine laying concrete
where there used to be gardens and roses?

Can you imagine having lord knows how many people living
in the same neighbourhood
and all speaking the same language
and yet, ninety percent of the time, most of them never even
acknowledge each other's existence

It's messed up, isn't it!

The Priest of St Jude's

The Priest from St Jude's was on my case today;
the sarcastic son of a bitch.

Honestly. it's ridiculous with this guy.

When he's in here alone, he won't say a thing to me.

Won't even look me in the eye most of the time!

And, same story when he's out there with fellas on the streets too.

In fact, you'll see him sooner cross the road or dive into a corner shop than walk past the fella in the gutter, begging for a little spare change.

But then, on a day like today – when he's in here having lunch with a few members of his little congregation (and they're buying!) . . . suddenly, the guy's on full saint mode.

He says;

"Vinny . .. my friend.
It is Vinny – right?
Yes, of course, I think I remember you coming to our Christmas service
a couple of times before.
Well now, how have you been?
I've not seen you in church for a while.
Still cleaning floors for a living? That's so good for someone like you.
Bless you for doing such a wonderful job of it.

*In fact, if you're ever free for some volunteering, we could certainly use
a bit of help with polishing the chandeliers in our building.
But you know — there's no pressure, of course.
It would just be lovely to see you at a service again sometime soon.
Perhaps this Sunday, if you have the time?
We're doing a lot of special events at the moment and . . . something
tells me that God has a message for you."*

Then he looks at me with those violently insincere eyes– as
all his little lunchmates are looking on in awe behind him.

And I'm just stood there
thinking:

*Oh — ok. Really?
God's got a message for me huh?
And he needs me to come to you for the translation?*

*Or, even better, he needs me to clean your church as a "volunteer" . . .
when I'm barely making rent working 16 hours a day on salary here?*

My man — you must be on dogfood!

*Trust me; if the good Lord's got something to say to me . . . I'm pretty
sure he knows where I am.*

Seriously — I'm not that hard to find.

And, if I happen to prefer spending my Sunday mornings in a dirty café, serving my community, cleaning up after all the low-life's of this town, instead of sitting in church . . . then, so be it.
This is where God sent me.
And you better believe I don't need polished chandeliers – stained glass windows – "voluntary donations"– or the help of some crook with a book, in order to find faith out here.

So, go ahead; you just keep on using that donation fund of yours to take another holiday . . . or buy another Rolex . . . or get those teeth of yours whitened again.
Because if you were really out here doing God's work, you and your little crew would spend less time locked away in that church "speaking" about salvation . . . and more time out there on the streets helping people who actually "need" salvation."

Yeah. That's exactly what I wish I could say to this guy.

If only I had the courage.

But, in the end; I know it's not worth it.

My mother always told me there are two kinds of people in this world who you can never have a rational conversation with;
Those with belief.
And those without it!

So, after he said his little piece, I just held my tongue for a
moment,
and replied something like

"Oh – sorry, father. I'm working this Sunday."

Then, with a sigh, The Priest just shook his head.
saying
 "Well – I wish you all the very best, Vinny"
(When, really, I've no doubt he meant *"Well . . . I've tried my
best, Vinny. Perhaps the Devil will have a cleaning job for you
instead"*)

And with that, he headed on out the door – closely followed
by his little lunch crew, who all took the opportunity to turn
their noses up at me.

They didn't leave a tip.

They never do.

And I thought these people were supposed to be out here
loving their neighbour . . .

Not judging us!

Cleaning

Everyone needs a reason to keep on living in this world.

And if mine happens to be cleaning, then just what is so wrong with that?

Sure – I'm well aware that this game is not exactly going to make me a millionaire.

And a couple of times, people in here have even said to me
"Vinny – you're wasted, man.
You seem like a smart guy . . . you should go to college.
Get a degree.
Or – at least try for a proper job? Because, you know, you're too good to be just a cleaner"

But, I wonder,
what does that even mean . . . *"too good to be a cleaner?"*

What, you think this job is only for "bad" people?

And that those of us who clean for a living are somehow "worse" than those of you who make the damn mess in the first place?

I mean, for real; do you think I'm just out here working my ass off for no reason at all?

For the sheer hell of it?

Just to waste another little bit of my precious life?

Honestly, the snobbery you get from people! It's just crazy. And it's not just from rich folks either!

I get this shit from drunks and wasters too.
In fact, they're even worse for giving out unsolicited advice; telling me exactly how I should be living my life. . . because, clearly, they've made such a success of their own so far!

You know, sometimes, I find myself thinking
"Man, it's like damn near everyone that comes in here has more of an opinion on my life than I do!"

And yet, did anyone ever stop to consider that I might be in this game because I *enjoy* it?

Because, surely – that's a possibility too, right?

I mean, that would be a much more logical explanation for why I'm out here breaking my back every day for less than minimum wage. . . and why I'm never late in the morning. . .and why I always work overtime in the evening. . . and why I don't ask anyone for credit, or tips. . .

Yeah, cleaning is more than good enough for me, thank you!

And sure, I first got into it because I didn't have much choice. But you want to know the real reason why I stay in it after all this time?

Because it makes me feel useful.

And I like being the kind of guy who will do all the jobs that no-one else wants to do.

And I take pride in trying to make the dirtiest places look a little nicer.

And I care about this community.

And I get to learn from people – even if it's just overhearing conversation

And it gives me a sense of purpose.

Something to wake up for.

Something to achieve.

Something to rely upon each day - knowing that no matter what week, month, or year it is, there's always going to be something out there that needs cleaning.

See what I mean?

There are a thousand reasons why I want to be in this job.

And yet, still, these people say

"Yeah, but . . . it's all so disgusting! You really should be doing better!"

The story of Leo

Look at that.
11am, and the world must really be waking up now –
because here comes old Leo; hobbling along with his little
fluorescent shopping bag.

Seems like he's on the vodka today, with that bottle in his
hand. And still wearing his winter coat too, though it must
already be 20 degrees out there in the sun.

Damn, my heart goes out to this guy.

God only knows what he's done to his leg!
He never used to limp like that.
And it makes a change for him to be so quiet too.
Usually, he's cussing or babbling about something; while
everyone else can only look on, wondering what on earth is
going on in that head of his.

I remember the first time I ever saw this guy; he was laid out
on a bench down by the river – legs spread all over the place
– clutching an empty whisky bottle like a kid with a rattle –
and having a full-blown argument with about six people . . .
even though there wasn't a single soul around.

It was almost impressive.

And ever since that day – he's just fascinated me.

I mean – where does he come from?

Where does he sleep at night?

How far does he walk in a day?
(Or, rather, how far does he limp?)

Where does he find the money to get so blazingly drunk?

When was the last time someone sat down and had a chat
with him?

When was the last time the poor prick even knew what day
of the week it is?

I'd love to ask him.
But he never seems to stop anywhere for too long these
days.
And, even when he does, I hear he can get a bit violent if
approached by a stranger.

In fact, I'm not even sure if Leo really is his real name.
 It's just something I heard him crying out once.

"For fuck's say, Leo!!"

Right as he tripped up a curb, and fell into a car wing mirror.

But whatever his name is; I think what breaks my heart the
most with this guy is that I bet he's got such a story to tell –
and yet, not only has he got no-one to tell it to,
but the likelihood is he's so far gone by now,
maybe he doesn't even have the ability to tell it anymore.

So, whatever he might have once needed to express, is now
forever locked inside.

And, I can't help thinking;
What if that's all he ever needed?
Just someone to talk to!

Someone who would actually care enough to listen,
so that he could share a little insight into whatever it was
that tore him apart like this;
because I guarantee,
there's no way he's always been out of his mind.

He might have been a good-looking guy once – or intelligent
as hell – with friends, family, and all the potential in the
world.

He probably had plans for the future.
Ambitions.
Dreams.
Everything.

And then, one day,
I guess something just
snapped.

Though what it was exactly, god only knows!

Maybe he was a gambling man, who took a loss that he could never quite recover from.

Or, maybe it was a failed career.

Or a hope that let him down.

Or grief.

Or betrayal.

Or a lover who broke his heart.

Maybe there was a time when he thought everything was going to be ok.
And then, days passed –
and months passed –
and years passed –
and he slowly realised that . . . No.
Things were never going to be ok again.

Ever.

Wouldn't that make him seem more a victim of this world than a villain?

Losing it

I wonder if I'll ever end up totally losing the plot one day.

I mean, when you watch the people in this city close enough
– you realise that everyone is a little bit insane anyway.
So, if we're all hanging by loose threads in this life –
then it's not out of the realms of possibility for any of us to
just fall off the edge here.

And trust me . . . with shit I've witnessed in the past, I know
full well I'm probably closer to that edge than most.

But this is the craziest thing to consider.

Because, actually; if I ever did end up like poor old Leo –
then the joke of it all is that I'd probably never even know
about it!
(Or, at least, I'd likely be the last to know!)

After all, it takes certain degree of sanity to even notice your
own insanity. Right?

The mad man never believes he's mad.

So, who's to say it won't happen.

Who's going to tell me if it has happened?

Who's to say it hasn't happened to me already?

God, just imagine that!

I might be sat here, right now – writing my little lines –
completely out of my goddam mind –
yet, still convinced that I'm getting along fine!

Ahh . . . who knows!

Maybe it's time I just get back to work and stop scaring
myself with this shit

Otherwise . . . even if I'm not insane already –
I'll probably send myself that way soon enough!

Out of place

I have always had this feeling of being somewhat out of
place in this world.

Kind of like being the only moth at a butterfly party

Or the dice player who ended up at a card table.

Or like the flower that tries to bloom on the front doorstep
of the Silver Spoon around this time every year.

Lord knows what kind of flower it is!
I've never really been able to identify it in any guidebook.

All I know is, the little thing pops up for a couple of days
- and then, very quickly, just seems to retreat right back into
the concrete again
as if to say
"Woah, no way! I'm not hanging around in a dump like this!"

*

If only I had my own little bit of concrete too.

Maybe I would do the same.

The Black Bricks

Something that has always really caught my attention in this neighbourhood is that a lot of the houses are made with black bricks.

It's something I noticed years back – even before I worked here. And to this day, whenever I go for a little walk around the block, I tend to stop a moment to admire these places; because I love it when people try to give the area a little bit of personality!

It's like, almost everywhere else in this city – the houses are just what you'd expect.
You've got terracotta brick – grey brick – stone – white walled – and, if you're lucky, the occasional painted pastel.
But, in all cases, the whole vibe is generally pretty forgettable.

Whereas, when it comes to these black brick places,
It's a different matter entirely!

They have such a presence about them.

So classy (in an ominous kind of way).

And I can't help wondering about who's idea it was to first make them like that?

I mean, if it was the architects or the builders who did it,
then salute to those guys!
I just wish they'd have carried on with adding a bit more
character to the rest of the city too.

Or, if they weren't built that way from the start – then I
wonder which family painted their house first . . .
Because everything has to start from somewhere, right?

So, for real, who's idea was this?

Personally, I've always liked to imagine that maybe the
houses once belonged to a bunch of artists.
Or occultists.
Or gothic novel writers
All of whom met up one day – (maybe even over drinks in
the Silver Spoon Café!) – and decided they'd all like to put a
new little twist on this dirty neighbourhood.

Yeah.
That would be nice, wouldn't it!

A story like that would really put a bit of value in this place.

But sadly, I happened to hear something about these black
brick houses earlier on today . . . and don't think I'll ever be
able to look at them quite the same way again.

*

It came from listening to a talk by this little tubby guy who was leading a tour group around the neighbourhood.

Apparently, they were on a "murder mystery" tour – i.e paying good money to have some little know it all lead them through the rough end of town, and scare the shit out of them!

But actually, it made a nice change to have a bit of a scholar arrive at our doorstep. So, I couldn't resist taking a break for a while to listen in on what the guy was saying.

At first, he was talking about St Jude's – where the group had obviously just visited – and referencing all the "evil spirits" that were said to inhabit there. (At which point, I thought "*Yeah . . . one of them is the priest!*")

He then also mentioned the tower block just over the other side of the park – which was apparently built on an old burial ground for plague victims. (*As if the neighbourhood couldn't get any more appealing!*)

And, sure enough, he had a lot of interesting things to say about The Silver Spoon Café too –particularly how it used to be a flop house back in the 1800s, with a reputation for a number of visitors mysteriously disappearing after *"being led to the room in the basement"*

Here, I should probably have stopped listening to be honest.

Or, if I 'd had the time, I should have interrupted, saying;
*"Woah, steady on my man! Some of us have got to go clean in that
basement later, so can we not go into how many bodies might be buried
under the floor please!"*

But as always, the conversation moved on too quickly. And,
before I knew it, one of his little group members was asking
him about some of the other houses they'd been noticing
on their walk so far too.

"Is there any significance to them having black bricks?"

With that, the tour guide just smiled – and took a moment
to open this question up to the rest of the group; seeing if
any of them knew the reason why these particular buildings
were all coloured black.

Was it something to do with the plague victims again?

No

Was it to cover up dodgy brickwork?

No

Was it anything to do with artists / occultists?

I didn't have a chance to ask.

Clearly, the guy was already bursting to explain things for
real.

And with a happiness that only comes by knowing a fact
that no-one else has guessed – he revealed that these black
bricks were not actually a design feature at all.
Rather, they were *"Simply the product of Father time".*

In other words (as he went on to explain) the buildings
should really still be a light grey colour – made with the exact
same bricks you see in the wealthier neighbourhoods.

But, over the course of the last hundred years or so –
with all the traffic,
and exhaust fumes,
and smoke,
and dust,
and smog,
and sweat,
and blood,
and blasphemy,
and general city grime that has been constantly increasing in
this area –
things have changed.

And the bricks of the houses here have slowly been dyed a
jet black – literally, as a result of all this crap sticking to
them!!

*

Man, I swear –
that might just be the single most disgusting thing I've ever
heard!

To think that there were no artists involved.
No inventive architects
No genius designers.

Nothing.

Instead, the houses all look like that because this entire area
is so damn dirty . . .and, in all these years, there isn't a single
other soul out there who has cared enough to do anything
about it!

Honestly, I don't think I'll ever sleep again.

I mean, what the hell was this guy thinking – just casually
dropping bombshells like that for everyone to hear?

Oh, sure . . . whisper it quietly to your little group of tourists
if you really have to.
They're not from around here.
They can handle it.

But for guys like me who actually have to live and work in
this area – don't you think it's a bit inconsiderate?

Why can't you just lie about it?

Make up a story.

Anything you like – if it'll help with believing that the whole
place is prettier than it really is!

Because for real — there are some things in this life that a man just really doesn't need to know!
And, while *"potential dead bodies in the workplace"* should be top of that list — it seems like *"neighbourhood wallowing in a hundred years' worth of filth"* might just be even worse!

*

How the hell am I going to be able to walk past those houses again later?

Ugliness

Isn't that just the way this life always goes!

Right at that moment when you genuinely believe you've got something beautiful - reality comes around to remind you that, fundamentally, everything is all pretty damn ugly underneath!

And now, what's left?

Where do we go from here?

How can someone like me even hope to make a difference, when he's working against an entire city of people who just couldn't care less!

It hurts, man. That's all I can say. It just hurts.

One minute, you really do think
"Wow . . . people are genuinely trying to make the best of this place

And then, before you know it, that naivety turns to
"For the love of God – does anyone else actually give a shit about anything at all!?

Cleaning the City

Day to day, I work three different beats at the moment.

The Silver Spoon Café is where I'm on salary (Whenever they decide to pay me)

Then, I also take care of the park across the street
 (Bins, grass, plants, pavements, toilets – the whole package!)

And, if I have time, I do a little curb sweeping or litter picking about 100 metres up and down this street too. (To be honest, more-so in the direction of the brothel than towards the church . . . as the Madame there actually pays me in tips sometimes – whereas the priest and his little congregation tend to just pretend they don't see me)

I also did a bit of door to door work this week – knocking on a few of those black brick houses, just to see if I could offer any help in cleaning them up.

But, sadly, most of the people in these places were pretty unenthusiastic about the idea.

I think I must have tried about forty or fifty doors overall – and only two of them bothered to give me a response.

The first was: *"Mind your damn business!"*

And the second was: "*Go to hell!*"

So, I guess that little ambition will have to wait a while!

To be fair though, it's probably a good thing.

Obviously, I still can't stand the thought of those buildings remaining so damn dirty – but, I already take on more work than I can handle anyway. And it's not like I'm getting any younger out here.

Trust me, though – if there were more hours in the day;
or if I could only have more than just this one life to live;
then maybe I could actually make a real difference.

I swear, I'd be out there cleaning up this entire block.
Maybe even the entire city!
Streets
Houses
Cars
Buildings.
Windows,
Toilets
Sewers

Everything.

I'd make the place so damn sparkling, that even the drunk in the gutter would have a shiny floor to collapse on.

Around my way

That's the problem around here. people just don't care
enough.

Sure, everyone is always moaning about how this place is
getting worse with each year.
And, to a certain extent – they're right.
In a lot of ways, it's getting pretty damn horrendous.

Yet still; who's fault is that?

Is it the buildings,
or the pavements,
or the boarded-up windows
or the graffiti
or the broken streetlamps
all doing this to themselves?

Or, does the problem really lie with the people instead;
These ones who see so much, and do so little!

Things could change

See, change is not that hard, really.

It's only when you're trying to do it *alone* that it becomes a bit more complex.
Because, as a collective, there's really not much that can't be achieved.

So, if absolutely everyone in this area really did get together one day and decided to make the place a little nicer, or a little friendlier – don't you think things could change pretty much overnight?

I mean, sure, it's not like we're make ourselves any richer like. I'm not saying we'd make a damn paradise here!

Chances are, we'd probably still be one of the poorest area of the city (at least, in financial terms).
And of course, we'd still have a hell of a lot of black brick buildings to be working on!

But, in terms of just achieving different kind of riches– making a neighbourhood where people genuinely take pride in the little that we do have . . . and do everything possible to make this place safe enough for everyone . . . in theory, there's really nothing stopping us!

We could make it like that any time we wanted.
Just by a change in attitude.

But . . . I don't know
Maybe it's just the laziness in people that prevents it all.

Everybody wants things to be clean.
But nobody wants to clean it for themselves.

Where will you be in 5 years?

Sarah in the café says to me today *"Vinny, where do you think you'll be in five years' time?"*

And I replied
"Honestly – I'll be lucky if I've got 5 months left in me the way things are going.
So let me just concentrate on making it to the morning for now, and we'll see what happens after that."

I mean
Do I want five more years?

Absolutely.

Lord knows, I'd go for five hundred more years if I could –
given how much work I could get done with that much time ahead of me

But, just being realistic–
living is a gamble.

No day is promised.
and no-one ever knows what's going to happen to anybody.

So, when that's the way it's always going to be here - I'm really not the type to sit around making predictions.

Even just thinking about the time I've been working in The
Silver Spoon - I've seen it all.

Some people living too long.
Some people dying too soon.

Some bad things turning out for the best.
Some good things going so wrong, it's almost unbelievable.

I see the weirdest things happening on a daily basis . . .
and surprises happening ten times more often than expected
outcomes.

So, when everything is so consistently inconsistent – it just
proves my point.
Life is flaky.
And you can't waste time trying to make real plans with it.

Let's be honest; if God gives me breath for another 5 years,
I'm exactly the kind of guy who could probably end up
down and out, sleeping in a doorway at some point.

But, for now at least
I'll settle for just staying where I am

Dirt is Dirt

Dirt is still dirt
No matter if you're cleaning a palace or a gutter.

And people are still people
Regardless of what they're doing with their life.

So, forget all this trying to choose between the good and the
bad.

At the end of the day, it doesn't matter where you are, or
what you're in to.
As long as you're trying to make the place better – that's
about as much as you can do

The story of Robbie

When I was sitting out front of the café this morning, I saw
a father calling out to his little son

The kid must have only been around 6 or 7 years old.
But you could just tell that he was out here taking his father's
soul today.
And this was probably the first time the two of them were
really going man to man.

"Robbie!!" the Dad yells
"Come here. Right now!"

But . . . the kid doesn't budge.

"Robbie!!" The Dad goes again
"Come here. I'm not playing games"

And he clicks his fingers
But, still, the kid doesn't move.

Clearly, Robbie's not playing games either

"Right" says the Dad "I'm going to count to five. And, I'm
warning you– If you're not by my side, it's going to be big
trouble, young man . . . You hear me?"

Oh, yeah. the kid hears him alright!

"You ready?"

Robbie smirks – like he's heard this a hundred times before

 "Ok then" The Dad says "Here we go.
"One . . . "

The kid doesn't move

"Two . . ."

Doesn't even flinch

"Three . . ."

Nothing

"Four . . ."

Still nothing

And now,
Everyone can see
The Dad is really starting to sweat.

For a moment, he even turns to look at me – as if to say
"This little sonofabitch has got me this time.
What am I going to do?"

But, having never been a father myself, I've got nothing to
offer him either

So, he quickly turns back to the kid again
And, he seethes
"Don't push me, Robbie. I'm warning you!
Now, I'm going to call it four and a half.
And if you don't come here this instant, I'll . . ."

He never gets the chance to finish the sentence.

Suddenly, little Robbie's mum comes gliding along,
seemingly appearing out of nowhere, like a vision in her
flowing overcoat.

And, instantly, the mood all changes.

"Is everything ok?" she says, glancing back and forth at the
two of them, like a sheriff interrupting a shootout.

And, you can see, the poor Dad wishes he could just be
honest with her

If there was any real sympathy in the world, he'd say
something like
"No, of course it's not ok!
Your boy here is being an absolute obnoxious little prick today"

But – the guy's a realist too. And he knows that honesty is
not always the best policy in a situation like this.

The kid will see him as a grass. . . meaning he'll make life hell for even longer.
And as for his wife . . . . she'll just lose all respect for him, thinking
"Who is this idiot?!
Not even man enough to deal with a seven-year-old!"

So, with a sigh, he knows he's a king caught in check. And, by the smirk little Robbie has on his face, the kid knows it too.

"Yeah" The dad stutters, eventually "Of course everything's fine. No dramas. We were just . . . waiting for you"

And, with that, the mother sweeps her little angel into her arms. Kissing him on the cheek.

"Oh, I'm so glad to hear that. You really are such a good boy, Robbie darling. How about we ask Daddy to take us for an ice cream as a treat – would you like that?"

Of course, Robbie nods his head gleefully
"Oh, yes please"
With just about the sweetest smile you'll ever see

Then, the two of them head off together.
Robbie hand in hand with his mother; leading the way in front of the poor dad, who just trundles along behind.

And it's at that very moment, with everyone in the entire city knowing full well who the man of the house really is

now . . . the kid manages one last quick glance back at his
father.

He says nothing.
But, by his eyes, you see exactly what he's thinking.

"Check mate, sucker"

Meditation

When washing dishes, it's funny how everything seems to let out these terrible cries and piercing screams if you handle it all roughly

Whereas, if you wash the stuff with a little more care – the noise of clanging and banging sounds something closer to the gentle tinkling of bells
As if all the plates and pans are laughing with each other!

*

To be honest, there's probably a lesson for life in there too.

You know – treat everything with care, and all that jazz.

But, sadly, in all my years in this job, I have found that what works with pots and pans doesn't always work so well with people!

You always run into someone

One of our old regulars in here once said to me
". . .see, that's the thing, Vinny.
A man can never escape his own past - no matter how much time goes by.
And, especially in a city like this; with all these people coming and going. It's as good as guaranteed that you will always bump into a familiar face somewhere.

Maybe it'll be your ex-girlfriend at a late night bar
Or your childhood friend at a bus stop
Or your old school teacher in a strip club
Or your preacher coming out of a back-alley whorehouse
But, trust me . . . this world is a lot smaller than you think.
The moment you think you've forgotten someone . . . that's exactly when they'll turn up again"

And you know – he's right.

It's situations like that which not only make me believe in God . . . but, also, have me convinced that he's got one hell of a sense of humour.
Because it's not just the fact that you always run into someone –
it's that you always run into them in the most awkward places too.

But, that being said, I've seen enough in here over the years to know that serendipity comes in many other forms too.

From the sublime, to the ridiculous.

For example, we had a guy in here earlier today accidentally spilling a drink on someone who turned out to be his long-lost cousin!
And I swear, I've never seen two fellas go from the brink of a fist fight to being best friends so damn quickly!

So, this is exactly why it's always worth sticking around in this life for as long as you can!
Because you just never know who is going to show up again at any moment.

Maybe that old friend you lost contact with all those years ago will call you up out of the blue one day.

Or maybe that love you lost . . . the *"one who got away"* . . . will turn up in a shop somewhere. And you'll ask them out to dinner – just like old times.

Honestly, in a city like this, anything is possible.

The story of Marco Durant

If there's one person in this world that I would love to meet again, it would be Marco Durant.
One of the only men in my life that I'd ever have classed as a real friend.

I remember, we first met on the rooftop of a skyscraper; back in the days when we both worked for a window cleaning firm which used to cover most of the office blocks in the financial district.

I was 2 weeks in to the job, about to do my first abseil down the side of the building to cover the top two floors.
And Marco, God bless him, was on support.
Literally, holding my life in his hands for the entire morning, until we switched places later for the afternoon.

So of course, in a situation like that, you tend to get pretty close to your work mates pretty quickly. And it helped that we were both from Albania – so the language barrier was never an issue.

But with me and Marco – it soon became something much deeper that just hanging out with each other due to proximity.

This guy could talk all day – literally from sunrise to sunset. And, the moment he realised that I could listen all day too,

I guess we both felt like we'd found something of a soul mate.

So, over time, we'd spend days on end just talking about every damn thing under the sun; from science and religion, to slot machines and pretty girls.
And then at weekends, (seeing as we both enjoyed a bit of a gamble) we used to link up with a few other guys from our team and head either to the casino or to the race track together.

Crazy, isn't it?

You'd think we'd have all had more than enough of gambling by the time the weekend came, given that we spent most days dangling hundreds of feet above the city on half broken ropes.

But, then, everyone needs a hobby – right?
And, as far as vices go, I always thought gambling was the best of the bunch.

At least we weren't just drinking or smoking our wages away, like other guys might.
And, every so often, one of us might just get a little win too, which always brightened up the week.

The only thing was – the more time I spent with Marco, the more it became apparent that he really didn't have much luck when it came to the gambling game.

Sure, he might have been by far the most intelligent guy I've ever met – but, no matter how high of an IQ he had in that head of his; as soon it came to gambling (which, ironically, seemed to be the thing he cared about the most) this guy's luck was absolutely unbelievable.

I used to say to him
"Marco, either you smashed one hell of a lot or mirrors in a past life . . . or there's a Witch out there who has put a damn hex on you!!"

Because, honestly, there was no other explanation for it.

In 2 years, I think I saw him win three bets at most. And one of them was only because the croupier at the casino misheard him!

But to be fair, Marco always took it all in good humour. And the kind of philosophical guy that he was, it always seemed like he was more out here just to enjoy the game; not really bothering about wins or losses.

So, in that sense, he might not exactly have been *"happy go lucky"* – but, at least, I could say he was "happy *no* lucky". And when I look back now, the only time I ever got a sense of something else going on within him, was on that final time when we were all at the races together.

The Track Day

It was a pretty regular Saturday at the time.
With Me, Marco, Gio, and a few others, all at the track to catch this month's steeplechase.

We were coming to the end of another expensive day for poor old Marco; so, as we were heading to place final bet, he told the rest of us that he was going to *"hedge a little bit"* for the final three races.

In other words, this meant that he was going to back the favourites in each race; but he'd be placing an *"each way"* bet too, rather than just going flat out for a win.

So, as long as his horses placed either first second or third in their respective races, he'd at least be able to walk away with some semblance of a success.

Now of course, this kind of wager wasn't exactly going to make Marco any kind of millionaire.

In fact, even if he won all of these last races outright, he'd still be nowhere near recouping even half of the money he'd blown already that afternoon.
 But I guess it was more about poor Marco trying to pull a bit of dignity back than anything else.
So, I didn't blame him for trying to stack the odds in his favour a bit.

Even now though, I can't believe what ended up happening in those final three races.

The 15:41 – Marco's "sure fire winner" has an unusually slow start, and never quite makes up the distance. Finishing fifth place

The 16:08 – Marco's horse is up top, battling for second - but gasses out on the final stretch and finished fourth

The 16:37 – Marco's horse leads for three quarters of the race. So far ahead of the others, it's almost unfair.
But then, on the final jump, the horse stumbles.
Goes down with a broken ankle.
Never gets up again.
And that was the end of it.

Lord knows who won that last race in the end.
Frankly, none of us cared.

We just watched the ambulance truck trundling on to the track to pick up the jockey.
And then, turning around to Poor Marco again,
it was hard to know whether to laugh or cry for the guy.

You could see the realisation suddenly hitting him
of all the money he'd lost that day.
And I felt so bad when he just shook his head, saying *"How on earth am I going to explain this to my wife when I get home?"*

 But, to be honest – I laughed so hard about it too.
We all did.

And, to be fair, by the time we were driving home a few hours later, even Marco was back to his normal self again, having a little joke about it all too.

I always remember that self-deprecating smile of his, when he said
 "Well, boys – there's a lesson here for us all.
Next time . . . always hedge on the second and third favourites too!
And also, never trust a grey horse!"

To which, Gio replied
"Marco, we're just lucky you only put a bet on one runner in that final race. Imagine if you'd hedged by dropping money on every horse out there! You could have killed the entire field!!"

Then later, when we finally pulled up at the station to drop Marco off – he reverted back to the same speech he'd always give us on days like this.
"Anyway – in all seriousness, guys – I think I'm done with all this gambling game now. Can't keep losing money like this.
I better just call it quits for a while. Maybe take up golf or fishing instead. I need a cheaper hobby!"

And, as he cracked another smile, which seemed to say *"We all know that'll never happen!"*
I remember the last thing I said to him was;

"Yeah? Ok, then. Well, see you next week Marco"

The Loss

But I guess this is just the way these things always happen, right?

No matter who it is, or how much you care for them,
there's going to come a time when you have to say goodbye for real.
And, more often than not, you have no idea when it's going to happen.

Sure, you think that goodbyes are always written like in the movies – where everything has a habit of coming to a nice, neatly, packaged, finale.

You think you're going to be able to shake their hand
share a last embrace
and then watch the person walk off into the sunset, as you wish them all the best.

But the reality is, nothing ever happens like that.

In my experience, most good things just tend to softly slip away instead. Completely out of your control.

And then it's only when you look back again - maybe after years have gone by, and the facts have just started sinking in
– that you realise
"Man. that really was the end of it!"

You said *"see you next time. . ."*
But there was no more next time.

It really did finish – there and then.
Never to return.

And this is kind of how it happened with poor Marco.

I remember, the following Monday he didn't turn up for
work.
Completely out of character for the man who was always
first on site every morning, without fail.

And the next day – same thing. Marco was a no show.
So, a couple of us who were closest to him started doing
whatever we could to try and track him down.

We left messages on his phone with no response.
Called his wife, with no answer.
Stopped by his house – but lights were out, and his car
wasn't there.

And, as another day passed –
and another –
and another –
everyone was getting seriously worried.

We knew something bad must've happened;
but everyone was too superstitious to start speculating.

So we could only keep waiting, and keep trying his phone.
Hoping that things would somehow still work out ok in the
end.

Then, finally, we reached Saturday again.
And, early in the afternoon, I get a knock at my door.

It was Gio. Accompanied by Marco's wife, Katrina; who
looked just about as exhausted as anybody I have ever seen.

They came inside.
And I remember feeling such an instant sense of dread come
over me as I followed them through to my kitchen – I didn't
even ask them to take their shoes off.

"Vinny" Gio said, "Listen. I've gotta tell you something, and
it's not gonna be easy.
But before I try . . . did you happen to hear anything back
from Marco at all this week?"

No, I hadn't

"Not since Saturday, right?

No, nothing since Saturday when he got out of the car

"And do you know if anyone else has spoken with him at
all? Or seen him . . . maybe earlier in the week?"

The more he spoke, the worse my stomach was churning

"No. there's been nothing" I said "I would have told you anyway – you know that.
But . . . why?
What do you think has happened?"

Gio paused a moment, glancing at Katrina

"Gio." I said again. Sensing he already knew what had happened.
"Tell me. What's going on?
 Is he alright?

"Vin. . ." Gio said "Marco's been in hospital. He. . . had a breakdown."

With that, I just frowned

"A breakdown?"
"What . . . as in – something with his car?"

And Gio looked at me like I was literally the dumbest man on the face of the earth. (Which, thinking back on it now, I absolutely was!)

"No Vinny." He replied "As in, a mental breakdown.
The kind of thing that had him throw himself out of a window on Monday evening"

My legs nearly buckled

"What!? You're joking. Is he . . . "

"Still alive?" Katrina interrupted "Yes - thankfully.
The idiot jumped right out the window in the spare
bedroom, and ended up landing in the bushes in our back
garden. So, he's got a few cracked ribs, and a fractured ankle;
but, overall, he's not too bad. . . at least, not physically.
In terms of his mental state though . . . that's a whole
different story. I've never seen him looking so broken."

Poor Marco! I thought. *Doesn't even have enough luck to throw
himself out of a window correctly!*

"So – where is he now?" I said "Still at the hospital?"

"Yes" Katrina replied "I'm on my way to collect him this
morning."

"Can we come too?"

"I don't think so. Not yet – anyway.
Vinny – the doctors wanted to have him sectioned.
Said he was a danger to himself, and should not be left alone.
But I know he'll never cope with being put on the psych
ward.
So, I'm taking him with me down south to stay with my
parents for a couple of weeks.
And after that, I'm not sure what will happen. But I don't
think he'll be coming back to work again any time soon."

I just couldn't believe what I was hearing.

All this time, I'd been convinced that Marco was just having
a laugh with the whole gambling game; much like the rest of
us were.

But as Katrina went on to explain, it turns out his problem
had been going much deeper than any of us had imagined.

Apparently, the losses we'd been seeing him take were only
the surface level.
In his spare time, Marco had maxed out a dozen credit cards
in almost every betting shop in the city too . . .
pouring lord knows how much money into slot machines
and online card games.

On top of this, he'd been bleeding his savings account dry.
And had gone so far into his overdraft on three different
bank accounts, that, now, the boys in blue were looking to
repossess their house.

So, with all that bubbling away in poor Marco's head,
topped off by that final loss at the track too;
clearly, the guy just couldn't take it anymore.

And to this day, it's one of the things I feel most guilty
about.
Not just for being such an active part of his addiction; but
also, for joking along with him about it all; when I should
have seen that all those fragile smiles were really cries for
help.

I swore from then on, I'd never gamble again.

And I said to Katrina that as soon as Marco was well enough
for a visit, me and Gio would drive down to see him.
Literally – anything at all to help get him back on his feet
again.

But sadly, that time never came.

Maybe it was Katrina who decided it was for the best; that
Marco needed to be free from everything, and that me and
the rest of the guys were bad influences on him.

Or, maybe it was Marco himself, who wanted to make it a
clean break from all us so called "friends", because, clearly,
we'd let him down badly by not seeing the signs of his
addiction.

Either way, the result was that every time I would phone
Katrina over the next months, she just kept delaying.
At first, saying *"he's doing ok. . . just needs more time to get back
on his feet before seeing anyone."*
Followed by
*"We're staying here for another month, at least, Then we'll make a
decision"*

And then, one day, Katrina's phone just stopped ringing.
Around about the same time a "sold" sign appeared outside
Marco's old house.

From some of the other guys at work who'd also been close
to Marco, the rumours were that he and Katrina had either
bought a farm somewhere close to her parents –
or were moving overseas, to escape some of the shady
characters Marco had ended up taking loans from during his
time gambling

But, to be honest, it seemed like everyone had been told
something different about it all.
So the only thing I can say for certain is that clearly Katrina
(and/or Marco) really didn't want anyone to know where
they were going.

That's why, over the years, I've had to just learn to live with
the fact that even in amongst all the crazy Serendipity I see
in this city . . . the chances of ever running into poor Marco
again are pretty much non-existent.

We'll never have another day at the races together.
And we'll never have another early morning hanging from a
rooftop together.

But you know, I can only hope that, every once in a while,
my man might just look back on our friendship as
something more than just gambling games.

And on nights like these, all I can do is sit here and send a
prayer out for him.

Because truly, if there was ever anyone in this life who
deserved a little bit of luck for the future!

Thinking about Ghosts

It's weird the kind of people who pop into your head when
you spend long enough on your own.

I remember someone asking me a few years back
"Are you afraid of ghosts, Vinny?"

And I just replied
"Man . . . look in my eyes.
Can't you tell I'm haunted by a hell of a lot worse than that!?"

But the truth is
Being alone means that you're thinking about ghosts
constantly. And it's crazy the kind of things that can come
back to haunt you if you give them a chance.

Obviously, at first, it's all the people you'd expect.
Grandparents.
Parents.
Former Friends.
Ex-girlfriends.
That kind of thing.

But then
as time goes on
that loneliness just starts getting deeper.

And soon enough, you reach a point where you find yourself thinking of people you really should have forgotten a long time ago . . .
Or missing people you never even used to like before!

For example, there is a guy who used to drink in here a few years back.
Literally, the most pedantic person I think I've ever met.

He was the kind of guy that would rub half a pot of antibacterial gel on his hands before he ate anything, just because he didn't trust the way I cleaned the toilet sinks!

And, while he'd never worked a single cleaning job in all his sheltered ass life – you could guarantee that damn near every time he came in here, he'd have me a new piece of advice for me.
Saying that I wasn't scrubbing things correctly.
And didn't use the right cloths.
And wore the wrong gloves.
And that I should always wipe tables in a clockwise circular motion, as opposed to my *"unforgiveable"* anti-clockwise – which, apparently, was "the devil's handiwork"!

My god, I really could have strangled that guy at times!

And no wonder he ended up coming in here so often.
He'd probably been kicked out of every other place in town for being such a pain in the neck!

But you know, that was all such a long time ago now.

And, these days, I really must be getting soft.

 Because the way things have been recently
and with how long I've been on my own at this point

I honestly just keep on thinking;

 "Man. If only that pedantic guy would show up in here again someday.

*I'd love for him to come back one time and annoy the hell out of me
again like the good old days!"*

The old man in the window

There is another fella who's been on my mind a lot too. Someone I used to see for years, sitting right here in the window seat of The Silver Spoon.

Even before I worked in here, I used to walk around this area near on every day;
and each time I passed this place, he was always there.
Same time.
Same seat.
Same dirty cup of coffee in front of him.
Same trilby hat on his head.
Same look on his face – like a man who knew each and every mystery in this world, but kept them to himself just for the sheer hilarity of it all.

Over time, I came up with so many stories in my head about this guy.
Everything from him being an old mafia don . . . to a former treasure hunter . . . to an eccentric millionaire, who had a penchant for absolutely disgusting cups of coffee.

It became like my favourite hobby; thinking up a whole backstory for who he was, or how he'd come to be here.
But really, I think I just liked him for how reliable he was.

Every day
Same spot
Without fail.

I remember the morning I first noticed a cleaning job being advertised on the door; he was in here.

The day I came in to enquire about what hours they were offering; he was in here.

My first morning shift – when one of the waitresses happened to tell me that the old boy's name was Vinny, just like mine – he was in here.

But then, the very next day; when I came in to work with the sole intention of striking up a conversation with old Vinny as soon as I could . . . he never turned up.

And, every day since then,
for more than nine years at this point,
he's never been in again.
Never even been seen in the area again, as far as I know.
Though, to be honest, I might just be the only person out here looking for him these days.
(As the longest serving member of staff in here by some distance . . . no-one else knows, or even cares, that he existed back then.)

So, it's that same old running theme again;
I find myself just left in this position of wondering
"What the hell happened to this guy?"

Clearly, the city has just moved on without him.
And the world just keeps on turning.

And, perhaps even the window seat has forgotten his name
by now.

But for me; every time I come over here to his old spot –
tidying up after whatever clueless clown has been here this
time – I get these chills.
And something inside of me can't ever let it go.

"How can a guy that reliable just up and disappear like that?"

Surely, somebody else out there knows who he was,
or where he is,
or, at least, might have noticed his absence.

Or – what?
Am I the only one who seems to give a damn about this
kind of thing?

No way, man.
Surely, someone's got to know something!

This guy didn't just spring out of nowhere, and fall back into
oblivion!
His name was Vinny.
He'd lived a whole life, before he became "that guy at the
window"

So, what? Did he move out of town?

Did he find a different café, in a different part of the city,
and, these days, spends his time looking out of cleaner

windows, at a nicer view, with a better made coffee in front
of him?

Did he run away with a woman half his age, and go live on
a yacht?

Did he go into hiding?

Did he drop dead?

Or – did he simply see me cleaning up on that first day in
here, and think *"nah, man; I'm not sticking around anymore if
they're hiring idiots like this nowadays!"*

I only wish I knew

2 in the morning.

Closing time.

2 in the morning.

And this is right about the point when I'll find myself in here all alone; having a full-blown panic attack, just thinking about how absolutely everything and everyone I ever care about – including myself – will eventually disappear.

Crazy, isn't it.

In bars all across this city right now – people are out there enjoying themselves.
Living like there's no tomorrow.

And here I am
Just thinking
"Shit. What if there really is no tomorrow?"

Honestly – this life is just
too damn much for me sometimes.

It's always 2 in the morning

"How did everything come to this?

"Why am I here?

"Why are any of us here?

"What does it all mean?

"What have I done?

"Why was I born?

"What is this life for?

"What is love?

"Why does time just keep ticking by so quickly?

"Why do all these people keep disappearing on me?

"Is it my turn to go next?

"Who's gonna clean these floors and windows when I'm gone?

"Or . . . what if the floors and windows leave first? What if they abandon me too? What the hell do I do then?

"What if the morning never comes?

"It's bound to happen sooner or later, right?

"Good God . . . my life is half over, and I feel like I only just got here!

"There's so much I haven't done.

"So much that still needs cleaning.

"So many stories.

"But what can I do with such limited time?

"What can anyone do with such limited time?

"It's all too little.

"It's all too much.

"What the fuck is even real?"

Ahh . . . 2 in the morning

My whole damn life is
2 in the morning.

What is it worth?

Everything will pass away

Everything.

Absolutely everything!

Sure, you ask for one more day
But that will never be enough, will it?

By tomorrow night
You'll be asking for another
And another
And another after that.

Though you know full well
that everybody leaves something unaccomplished
and everyone has a wish that remains unfulfilled

So what the hell is all this worth, really?

Questions and Answers

Another day
Another dawn.
And, thankfully, the panic has subsided a little now.

Who knows what causes it all!

There's something about the darkness that brings
everything to light, I guess.
But whatever the reason; I need to get a handle on myself
again now.

If I was a smarter man, I would just mind my own damn
business with all of this, and just stick to cleaning.
At least then I'd actually make some progress in my day –
and definitely end up with a better night sleep at the end of
it too!

I mean, with cleaning, everything is simple.

Just scrub hard enough, and you'll get it eventually.

Whereas with life, it's a whole different thing.

Every time you work at something – you find there's more
work to do.

And every time you think you've finally got the world all figured out – something comes out of nowhere to start beating you over the head again.

So, maybe it's fine to have all these questions . . . but really not worth stressing over actually finding answers!

You know, I used to think I was pretty smart.

But nowadays, I know that I'm only just about intelligent enough to realise how dumb I really am.

To Live this life

Let me have the wisdom of a man who knows nothing.

And the joys of a man who has seen true despair.

And the courage of a man who is riddled with doubt.

Then I will live this life smiling through my tears.

And hoping through all fears

Staring Death straight in the eye,
and blowing him a kiss!

Calm it down

I don't know how things are supposed to be.
But I do know that this life doesn't have to be so goddam
dramatic all the time.

I mean, sure
Everyone likes a fairy tale, right?

Everyone likes a tragic romance
Or a suspense thriller
Or a touch of the opera.

But, here – we're in real life.
And, after a while, all those endless twists of fate are really
just irritating.

So, wouldn't it be nice to just live a life of simple, easy, work.

No more stresses.

No more pressures.

No more highs or lows.

I mean, it wouldn't be so bad, would it!

Parallels

If there is one similarity between life and cleaning
it's that despite their differences in complexity, in both of
them the work is never finished.

After all, it doesn't matter how many times you go through
this process of wiping, polishing, scrubbing, tidying,
spraying, rinsing, wiping again etc . . . you're never going to
get the thing 100% clean.

And, even if you get it to 99% - all it takes is a few days of
neglect, or one little careless accident, and you're right back
to square one again.

So, essentially, you're slaving away forever on a task that you
know damn well you can never fully complete.
And, in that way, isn't it just the same with life too; where
you're trying to find answers to something you'll never
understand!

But, here's the thing.
In a weird way, there's beauty in all of this too.
To think that we all just keep working away at things
anyway, regardless of whether we can actually fully complete
the task or not.

It's like, any old idiot can work hard at something when they
know there's a guaranteed result.

But it takes a special kind of idiot to work hard at something purely for the love of it, knowing full well that it will probably never reach a satisfactory conclusion.

We'll all leave this life with work still to do.
That much is guaranteed.

But the trick is to always just keep on working anyway; while we still have the chance.

The triviality of philosophy

Look at these people in here tonight.
All in their little groups of twos and threes.

Isn't it kind of hilarious to think about just how trivial all of
this is?

I mean, every single one of us has been born with the kind
of mind that could contemplate the whole damn universe, if
we wanted to.

So, you'd think that when we're all in a place together like
this, everyone would be philosophizing, right?
Comparing notes.
Talking metaphysics
Bouncing ideas.
Seeing what everyone else has uncovered about this
ridiculous life of ours.

At the very least, we should all be in a permanent state of
self-enquiry; trying to understand who we are for real – or
where this existence even comes from.

And yet, at this very moment.
None of that existential nonsense particularly matters to
anybody.

Life
Death

God
Deeper meaning

Maybe it's all something we might get around to thinking
about one of these days!

But for now, there are more important matters at hand
Like
"How do I look?"
"How's my hair"
"What's the time?"
"Have we started having fun yet?"
"Do my friends still like me?"
*"Am I the toughest guy in the room . . . or should I play the clown
instead?"*
"What does this person think of me?"
"What do I think of them?"
"What do they think I think about them?"
"What is everyone else thinking about any of us?"

It's all so self-centred, isn't it?

The longer the night . . .

And isn't everyone so carefree!

Or, at least, so good at pretending!

But – just let the night go on a little longer . . .
and look a little closer

The truth will always show.

The smiles are forced
The laughs are insincere
The masks are fragile
The words they speak are all just repetition and rephrased
clichés.
The handsome couples all have ugly relationships.

And look at what they're wearing too . . .
The jackets.
The shirts.
The fragrances.
The shiny shoes.
The Jewellery (fake or real . . . does anyone really care?)

Doesn't it seem like everyone might just be
overcompensating for something?

I mean, look at this guy who just walked in.

He's got arms the size of my legs, and a black T-shirt with
the gold badge of some brand (which must really be
important!).

He's got bracelets all around his wrists;
ripped jeans;
studded boots;
manicured beard;
slick hair,
eyebrow piercing,
tattoos running from his fingertips right the way up to the
side of his neck. . .

Man – for real . . . who are you trying to fool?

A goose is still a goose
No matter how you dress it.

No-one knows why

Happiness is as light as a feather
Yet, when it comes, it is so hard to hold on to.

Sadness is heavier than the earth
Yet, when it comes, we carry it everywhere.

That which is good, ends so quickly
That which hurts, never really heals

Life is given, from no-one knows where.
Life is taken . . . No-one knows when.

Light and darkness
Joys and pain
Hopes and fears
Fortune and misfortune
Creation and destruction
Dreams and nightmares
Life and death

Day after day - month after month - year after year

One thing follows another

And no-one knows why!

Half Magic – and Half Tragic

This street.

This city

This world.

It's all shadows and light.

It's love and hate.
Good and bad.
Right and wrong.
Saints and sinners.

Everywhere.

It's wealthy neighbourhoods on one side of the road,
and ghettos on the other.

It's millionaire penthouses
overlooking streets where people are starving.

It's all of the most beautiful things that humanity can
possibly create . . . shoulder to shoulder with the absolute
worst we can come up with too.

And it doesn't matter where you are, or what you do.
You'll see it all.

Nobody gets away with anything.

So, just like it's ridiculous to believe anyone who says that
the whole world is evil . . .
Same goes for everyone who says that it's all good here too,
or that everything works out in the end.

The fact is – sometimes it does.
And sometimes it doesn't.

Sometimes it's ugly.
Sometimes it's art.

This city –
This world –
This life –

It's all half magic
And half tragic.

There's nothing to do

Tonight
There's nothing to do.

The city that never sleeps
Is obviously taking a little nap for a while.

And there's nothing to do

There's nothing to do

There's nothing to do
but to wonder if you
are as fine
and as free
and as lonely
as me

Too Quickly

It all goes by too quickly, doesn't it!

I mean, when love comes, and then
Love has passed
And love is past
And *life* has passed
And wishes came true
And success turned out to be hollow
And dreams became memories
And friendships failed
And innocence became experience – but experience still
didn't bring about wisdom
And the waiting just went on
And on
And on
But the moment you were waiting for still never really came
So you just clung on to something
Anything
Everything
And yet . . . still

It all went by too quickly
Didn't it!

Who Knows?

Will the sadness, last forever?

Yeah
Probably.

But will there be moments of happiness to come too?

God, I hope so.

The story of Demani

Demani is a kid who's been coming in here for a while.

Well – I say he's a kid; he's got to be around sixteen or
seventeen years old by now.
But when you watch someone grow up like this, then I guess
they just stay fixed in your mind in a certain way.

So while Demani runs with a different kind of crew now –
for me, he will always be that the wide eyed little boy who
used to come in here every Sunday after church with his
grandmother.

They never ordered much. Maybe just tea and toast for
Nanna and a banana milkshake for little Demani.

But, I remember, the two of them were just about the only
customers in here who would actually clean up after
themselves before they left.
So, immediately, I liked them.
(You can tell a lot about a person by the way they leave their
table in a café!)

Sadly, I never really got to talk with his Nanna as much as I
wanted.

I mean, this woman had such an air of dignity about her, it
was crazy.
So to be fair we did pass the time of day together every so
often.
But it was only ever general day to day stuff, really.
Nothing major.

And to be honest, the one thing that Nanna liked to talk
about more than anything was not her own life anyway.
Rather it was how proud she was of her little grandson;
for getting on so well at school – and, more so, for how he
was quickly becoming the new star of the St Jude's church
choir.

Now, obviously, almost every grandmother in the world
thinks their kid is an angel;
So, when she first told me about her little singing sensation,
I didn't think much of it.

I'd been to a couple of concerts at St Jude's over the years
(admittedly, before Demani had gotten involved there) –
and, from what I could remember, it was not exactly a
heavenly chorus back then!

But one Christmas, it just so happened that the newly
revamped choir came out to sing carols in the park across
the road from here – right about the time I was on litter
duty.
 And, hearing the kid sing for the first time that day,
I remember immediately just thinking

"Jesus Christ — this woman just might be on to something here, with this whole thing about her kid being an angel!"

Because, honestly, there was no other explanation for it. Little Demani's voice was absolutely unbelievable.

So good, in fact, that he actually became a bit of a local celebrity for a while; with a couple of magazines around here writing of him as their own little prodigy.

And before long, people from right across the other side of the city started coming to concerts at St Jude's, just to hear the kid doing his thing.

Then one Sunday afternoon, I remember Nanna came bouncing into The Silver Spoon all on her own, with the most wonderful news to share.

Apparently, the principle from the National School of Music had been at the church that morning specifically to meet little Demani.
And he'd been so impressed, that he had offered the kid a place at their residential school.
Even saying that the school were willing to cover half the course fees for him too, under some kind of inner-city talent scholarship.

It was beyond a dream.
Both for Demani , and for Nanna.

The chance to finally escape the poverty he'd been raised in.

But the only problem was that even with 50% off course fees, Nanna still couldn't get anywhere near enough money together in order to afford the rest.

And, unfortunately, we all know that genuine charity can be hard to come by in an area like this. No matter the talent.

So, with too much dignity to resort to begging on the streets, and no way of convincing the principle to cover the full price for them as an act of good will – the only other option she had, was to talk with the priest at St Judes.

If he could write a letter of recommendation for them, then maybe the banks would reconsider her loan application.

Or, even better – maybe the church would even sponsor Demani themselves.
After all, he'd been bringing in so many donations over the last couple of years . . .
Clearly, they could afford it!

But – no.
The Priest was obviously not very keen on the idea of losing his little superstar.

So, when Nanna approached him,
he just told her that the church was *"regrettably not in a position to assist in individual financial matters"*

And, as for the letter of recommendation for the banks, he
said
*"I will of course help you with the letter if I can . . . just as soon as
God grants me a spare moment. You know, I do have an entire church
I'm trying to run right now too!"*

But believe it or not; at the time, Nanna took this response
as a glimmer of hope.

She was so sure that the Good Lord really would offer a bit
of spare time for The Priest to help her out.
Because, after all, he was a man of his word – right?
A man of the church!
Acting in the best interest of his congregation – encouraging
everyone to *"surrender to God's will and have faith"*

Yet, as the time went marching ever onwards –
still there was no letter.

And then soon enough,
the last application deadline just slipped away.

The Priest went on holiday; never returning any more of
Nanna's calls.
And Demani's space was just given away to someone else.
*(Probably some spoilt little rich rich kid, with half the talent, but who's
family could at least afford the full price fees!)*

Ridiculous, isn't it!

I felt like marching straight to St Jude's myself, and saying to that priest *"How the fuck can you be so callous!"*

But there was really no point.

Poor Nanna had already damn near killed herself trying to get him to give them a helping hand – there was nothing more that an idiot cleaner like me could help with.

And, besides, a greater concern was what would happen to Demani now – because, clearly, he was not taking this disappointment with the same grace as his Nanna.

In fact, almost overnight, it was like you saw his whole demeanour change; from bright eyed boy – to angry young man.

He was pissed off;
At his Nanna
at the school principal –
at the church –
at the priest –
at the city –
at the world –
at his life –

At *everyone*.

And, honestly – who could blame him?

When fate deals you this kind of hand – offering you a chance at just about the only dream you ever had, and then snatching it all away again simply because you're not from the right area – then is it any wonder that you react by just wanting to be out there putting a middle finger up at the whole damn world?

So, Demani quit singing.

And refused to church anymore.

And started hanging around the streets with a different kind of crowd instead.
The kind of guys who, for their own reasons, were probably just as disillusioned, and just as angry, and just as broken hearted, as he was.

Last year, the kid served his first stint in a young-offenders institute . . . for throwing a brick through one of the stained-glass windows at St Jude's.
(In broad daylight too! As if he wanted the whole city to know exactly who had done it!)

And though he's back out on the block again now, it's anyone's guess how long it will be before he's in trouble with the law again.

At this point, you get the impression that he just genuinely couldn't care less either way.

But for now, at least – here he is again.

Sitting at a table in here with two local tough guys – pretending that he's never been in here before – and ignoring the fact that, right now, the stereo is playing his Nanna's favourite song.

Tragic, man

Absolutely tragic.

Justice

It makes you wonder sometimes if there really is any justice
in this world.

When you've got guys like Demani and his crew out causing
chaos on the streets, it's too easy to just say
"These kids are no good!"
"You should lock them up and throw away the key"

But then when you start seeing what actually leads most of
them into this position in the first place,
you realise that they're far from the only ones at fault here.

The bigger problem lies with this selfish society,
where people are too quick to condemn,
and where everyone out here knows full well that things are
messed up . . . yet, still, the vast majority of people never do
a single thing about it.

Prayer

Lord, give me two minutes with Demani one of these days.

Just two minutes
where it's him and me in here on our own
with none of his other idiot crew around

I'll tell him
Listen, kid — enough of all this small-time gangster nonsense.

What? You think you're the only one who ever had a dream go wrong?
Or that no-one else is carrying their own heartbreaks?

Boy, don't be so naïve.
Look around. There's not a person out here who's life ended up exactly
as they hoped it would.

But what's the plan here?
Are you really gonna be like all these others?
Just letting your life go to waste, and screaming "fuck the world", as
you get yourself locked up in a cell again, or gunned down in an alleyway
for no damn reason?

Come on — you're better than that.
And deep down, you know it too.

You know damn well that your Nanna didn't raise you a fool.

So - go home

Go spend time with her again.

*Or, if you really are as big a man as you think you are these days —
then go use this "fuck the world" of yours as motivation to actually do
something better.*

Show all these people you can make it without their help.

Go sing on a damn street corner if you have to, and see what happens.

Just don't fade out like this.

You've got music inside of you.

Don't let it go to waste

*

Yeah
That's everything I wish I could say to him.

But, even if I did . . . I know he'd never listen

Frankly, when I was his age;
I wouldn't have listened to a guy like me either!

Other perspectives

What am I in the eyes of most people around here?

A fool?

A creep?

A weirdo?

So uncouth and awkward and all?

Am I on a par with the stains on these bathroom mirrors, or the grime that keep me company each day?

Am I the lowest of the low – being slave, not only to the rich folks, but also to the drunks and the good for nothings of this city too, who just leave their filthy rubbish all over the place, knowing that someone like me will have to clear it up for them?

Am I really so contemptible?

Well – fine.
That's no problem.

I'm not working here to achieve the admiration of idiots!

And, even if they are right.
Even if I really am the bottom of society.
The lowest of the low.

I would still clean these floors with the same care.

And I would still write these pages of mine.

If only as a way of showing what such a lowlife has in his
soul!

Home

When I first moved to this city,
I felt more at home here than I ever had in my own country.

I came for a better life;
smuggled in on the back of a freight truck.

And it helped that, when I first found work, I remained part of a little Albanian eco system too – with me, Marco, and Gio working alongside other immigrants from all over the place.

To be honest, that's probably why it took me so long to learn the language too.
At work, we never had a single English speaker.
And, outside of that, I was only ever in the company of Albanians.

But, not long after Marco left – I remember things really started to fall apart for us all; with wages not being paid on time, and other fellas in our little community leaving us on a weekly basis.

In that sense, I guess you could say my unlucky friend must have been our lucky charm.

And, if I'd been a smarter man, I should have seen the signs – maybe gone on to a different firm while I had the chance.

But, for whatever reason, I stayed. Probably convincing myself something like "better to just stick with what you know . . . than risk something unfamiliar anywhere else"

And then, exactly 5 years ago today, something happened which, for the rest of my life, I'll never be able to get over.

That day

The fella's name was Yuri.
A good-looking guy, originally from Israel; who had been hired in Marco's place as my new partner.

He was with us for the best part of three months. And while we never spoke much due to the language difference, I remember he always used to show up for work with this great smile on his face – as if he genuinely thought we were doing the best job in the world.

And looking back now, maybe it really was more than just a job for him.
Because as far as any of us could tell; the guy had no family, no friends, no girl, no guy – and, to be honest, no real interest in much of anything at all, other than just being out here in the open air.

So, I try to take consolation in that at least he enjoyed his time with us – or maybe he genuinely was living out some kind of dream out here.

But, realistically, even if I knew he'd been having the damn time of his life up there – I still don't think it would stop this thing from haunting me now.

That morning.

Late September.

Around 5 am

With our whole team on an early shift together.

Me and Gio were on the roof of the building, holding anchor.

Yuri was abseiling a few stories down – alongside Gio's partner Andres.

Of course, the ropes we were all using were those same old worn-out ones that Marco used to complain about so much.

But, as ever, we'd all been pretty rigorous in examining them that morning; and they were no worse than they had been the day before – when Gio and I had been on hanging duty.

So, everything was normal.

And, looking back now – that's what feels so surreal.
The sheer *normality* of it all.

Being stood there

30 stories high.

Sun rising

No breeze.

Team of workmates around me

City streets waking up beneath us

A couple of airplanes high up in the sky overhead.

It was the last time in my life that I ever felt like things really
were "normal"

And then . . .

Snap.

That most awful,
gut-wrenching,
life changing sound I have ever heard.

Snap

Just once.

But loud enough to shatter any heart who heard it.

And quickly followers by something even worse.

The sound of Yuri's piercing cry.

Echoing all around us – not so much of fear . . . but more so of just sheer surprise.

Immediately, I fell backwards – as if my legs couldn't understand why the weight they'd been bracing against for the last half an hour had vanished so quickly.

But, before I knew it, Gio had rushed over to help me up – having secured his own line. And then the two of us shot to the side of the roof again, looking down where our two friends had just been.

On my side, there was nothing but empty rope. With a section of caved in scaffolding some way below, which had obviously gone down with Yuri.

And on Gio's side - Andres was now hanging alone. Grey as a concrete. Looking up at us with there wild, terrified eyes –screaming

"Get me the fuck off this building!!!!
"Gio!! Pull me up!
The rope . . . he just fell.
Oh, God! He just fell!
Pull me up!!
Vinny.
Pull me the fuck up!!!!"

Gio unclamped his line again – and, together, we started hauling the guy up to us.

But my head was so gone at that moment, I damn near went right over the side of the building too.

So Gio pushed me away again – finishing the lift solo

And then, when Andres was finally safe, the three of us just ended up collapsed on the rooftop together.

Wondering how, after so much chaos, the morning air could still seem so damn silent up here.

Memories

In the days between Yuri's accident and the little funeral service we arranged for him – my emotions were totally shot to pieces.
And, in fact, it has been that way for me every day since then too.

Sure, everyone kept assuring me that it wasn't my fault.

The police and the fire brigade saw the security camera footage – and said it was all just a terrible accident.

Gio, Andres, and the other guys all said that it could have happened to any of us.

And my bosses did everything they could to assure me . . . and, more importantly, convince the building managers . . . that the whole thing was totally Yuri's fault.
That he'd been messing around on the line.
Or, for some reason, had purposely cut it himself
(Basically, any lie they could spin in the hope of saving the contract that they had)

But it was no use.

Whether lies, or truths – nothing could take away the fact for me that I was there.

I was the one who let Yuri on the first hang that morning.

I was the one holding that damn rope

I was the one who heard that terrible snap.

And, I'm the one who *still hears* it too. . . every night . . . right around the time when I should be dreaming.

So, frankly, this isn't even about whether it was my fault or not.

Guilty or innocent;
A man still has to carry his memories.

Aftermath

And Lord knows where any of those other guys are now!

Our bosses were supposed to be taken court over the whole incident – but they vanished pretty rapidly soon after the court summons.
And as quickly as that, our firm was closed – leaving our entire crew unpaid and out of work.

I think Andres moved somewhere up north, to work gardens instead of windows.

And Gio had a girl overseas; so she bought him a ticket to go out and see her.

But, as for the other guys in our team – who knows?

I guess they didn't hear that terrible snap . . . so maybe they were able to just carry on, and find the same work in a different firm.
Or to move on to better things.
Maybe bigger cities
Or ever larger buildings.

To be honest, there have been a few times in the Silver Spoon Cafe when I've seen guys come in for a quick coffee, and found myself thinking *"Man – you like mighty familiar"*

But, then again, there was an American guy in here just two days ago who, for a brief moment, had me thinking he was the splitting image of Yuri too.

So perhaps it's sometimes better to stop looking for familiar faces around here.

Otherwise, you risk seeing too much!

Future Past

When I started writing, I used to spend all my time talking about other people.

And yet, the more I write
The more I seem to talk about myself.

Strange, isn't it!

It's like the more we go one way in this life . . . the more it leads us in the opposite direction. And the further we travel from home, the closer we are to making it back again.

So, that's why they say a man can never outrun his own experiences, I guess.

The older you get
The more you reminisce.

The further you go into the future
The more you'll find yourself thinking about the past.

My Day

Young fella in here is talking about how he missed his bus
this morning, and ended up losing his job as a result of being
late.

He says to his friend
"Bruv – it's not been my day"

And I'm over here smiling to myself, just thinking

"Child, wait till you get to my age!

When you start to realise that it's not been your day
or your week
or your month
or your year

or your *life!*"

The pursuit of Happiness

Everyone wants to be happy in this life.

But the sad thing is, if you ask people directly; almost no-one seems to know what this thing called "happiness" even is!
So, in that sense, is it any wonder that people end up looking for it in all the wrong places?

It's like, the local drug dealer says you can smoke or sniff your way to happiness.

And the bartender says you can find it at the bottom of a bottle.

And the casino owner says you can win it at a card table.

And the magazines say it'll come when you finally look pretty enough.

And damn near the whole world seems to think that happiness is a transaction. So, the more money you have – the more happiness you get.!

But at the end of the day, nothing ever lasts for very long.

I see it all the time.
As soon as the high is over,
you just return to your former low.

And as soon as the money's been made,
you realise there's always just a little more you need to be
making too.

That's why I feel like the pursuit of happiness is more a
game of *waiting* than it is of *searching*.

I mean, there's always a chance that happiness doesn't exist
at all – and we're all just wishing for the impossible!

But, let's think positive.

If happiness really does exist – then I bet it's something that
will come along out of the blue to find us at some point.
Not the other way around.

And in the meantime, the best we can do is just try and be
ready for it. Kind of like waiting for a friend to visit from
out of town.

It's no good expecting happiness to come see you when
your home is a mess, and your life is even more so!

You've got to get up
Put the work in
Make the place look nice
Get your shit together.
And be someone who is actually *ready* to be happy.

Otherwise, who knows; maybe real happiness will come
calling at your door one morning – but, you'll be so hung

over from the night before that you won't even answer the call.

Or, even worse, what if you're there to meet happiness when it comes – but, as soon as it sees the state of your life right now, you'll see it turn itself back around again. Saying *"Good God – I'm not staying in a dump like this!"*

See what I'm saying?

Happiness is rare enough as it is; so if you can't even offer it somewhere clean to visit – you can rest assured it'll have plenty of other places to be instead.

She's priceless

Pretty woman in the café tonight

Trying to get my attention . . .
Just like she's trying to get *everyone's* attention.

Look at her,
all wandering eyes, and dangerous curves;
sitting there as if she just inherited the place.

She's dressed in next to nothing
but she's wearing it like it's
everything.

And she's got that air about her, where you can just tell;
this girl is priceless . . . but she treats herself like she's
worthless.

Such a shame, man.
Such a damn shame.

I bet she's spent hours getting ready tonight too!
Dolling herself up;
making herself "look the part".

I bet she does just about everything she possibly can –
probably because no-one's ever told her that she looks ten
times better without all the warpaint.

And you can guarantee that in a little while,
when she checks her look in the mirror again,
she'll only ever be looking skin deep.
Never once trying to see the beauty that might well just be
in her heart instead;
worth so much more than all this other nonsense she's
building her self-worth around.

Damn.

I wonder what would happen if I tried to talk to her about
some of this?

That would be a hell of a story, wouldn't it!

Imagine if she smiled at me . . . and I smiled back at her . . .
and I went over there . . . and we got to talking . . .
and we found we actually had a lot in common . . .
and the signs were all aligning . . .
and I . . .

*

Ahh – come on, Vinny.
Pull yourself together!

What are you gonna do;
Go over and offer to clean her table?

Man, trust me

She's not out here looking for a fella like you tonight.

And, anyway – even if she was, how do you think this is going to play out exactly?

You gonna buy her a drink . . . when you can barely afford your own?

You gonna drop the mop and ask her to dance?

You gonna put down your pen – close this book – hand over your heart to a total stranger once again – and give up on the whole works?

Forget it.

You know full well that fairy tales don't start in late night cafes!
And besides, a woman like that is out here looking for a good time tonight.
Whereas, you?
You're just out here to clean up after everyone, remember?

So, come on
Just stop with all these dumb ass ideas!
And if she looks at you again . . . just smile and look away.

This is no time for dreaming.

Fake confidence

I remember when I used to be more the type to approach woman like that.

When I was a younger man, I could fake a bit of confidence when I needed to.
Or stand tall – even when I was feeling small.

But eventually, the same old strains would start to show through again.
That voice inside, saying;
"Woah . . . slow down, Vinny.
This is starting to have potential now.
You sure you can trust them?
You sure this is for you?
You sure you can go through all of this again?
Because one of these days . . . they're going to find out what you're really like.
And that's not going to work out well for anyone, is it!"

Then, at that point, things can only ever go one way.

I'd start backing off.

Making excuses like
"Sorry.
Working late again.
Just don't have the time right now.
Will link up again with you soon"

And meanwhile, with a bit more time, the woman would be
thinking
"What the hell?
How is this the same guy I met to begin with?
Didn't he used to seem so secure?
Didn't he used to have something interesting to say?
Wasn't he a little more handsome when we first met?
Has he really always been a cleaner?"

Until, finally, the whole thing was over before it begun.

She'd say to me;
"Sorry Vinny. You're just not the person I thought you were"

And all I ever had in reply was;

"To be fair
I'm not the person I thought I was either!"

Showing up

The only thing I have ever been able to commit to fully, is work.

Why?

Because work is something to rely on.

And, cleaning is pretty much the one part of this life where I can actually make a positive difference!

See, in the vast majority of this life, I have a tendency to be pretty damn useless.

I couldn't spot the signs of Marco's gambling problem.

I couldn't prevent Yuri from taking his fall.

I couldn't do a thing to help Nanna, or Demani, or Leo – or anybody else.

But, at least here . . . in the worst end of town . . . in the dirtiest little café . . . I can make some kind of positive contribution.

No, I might not get the place as clean as a fancy showroom. But, there's comfort in knowing that it's still better than it would be if I wasn't here at all.

Builders

Crew of builders in the café this afternoon;
treading dirty rainwater all over my floors,
and making so much noise while they ate, you'd think they
were still talking over their damn cement mixers!

My God, these guys are obnoxious.

Oh, ok
I get it;
You built the apartment block just around the corner from
here, and now you think you own the whole place, huh?

Well – fine.
If that really is the case, then tell me,
what have you ever done for the people in that building
since then?

Because I don't know if you've noticed, but the place is
really not looking too clever these days!
And if you are the ones to build it; surely you'd want to take
a little pride in it too – helping to maintain whatever you put
there?

Or . . . is it just that you guys were doing it for the money?

Were you happy just to drop a few dodgy bricks; building
an apartment block that you know is gonna be vastly
overpriced for most people around here anyway?

And were you laughing when your cash had gone through –
knowing that, in a couple of years' time, the whole place will
need a big refurb again; and, you'll be able to send more of
your men over . . . for another half assed job . . . at double
the rate . . . just so that the rents can go up again, and the
whole shit show can continue.

Man – I really can't stand the attitude of these guys.

When they should be building houses to improve people's
lives – they use them to stand on the roof, and spit on us all
instead.

And, you can guarantee; at some point this afternoon,
one of these clowns (who, by the way, never even stop to
wash their hands before eating!) will have the nerve to look
around in here too, and say something clever to his buddies.

"Damn, this place is a real dump isn't it!"

"When are they gonna knock it down?"

*"I'd let it fall on half the people in here too . . . kill two birds with one
stone!"*

*

Oh really?

You'd let it fall on us all, huh!

Well – ok.

Give it a few years – it'll probably happen anyway.

And, until then – why don't you fellas just find somewhere else to make your mess in.

Because, do you know something?

This place is a dump – but it's still far too good of a dump for a bunch of fucking animals like you.

Different kinds of work

Nothing in this life is ever easy.

But, at the same time,
nothing is ever permanently difficult either.

Essentially, it's all just different kinds of work.

I see it all the time in the cleaning game.

Sometimes it's a good day, and you're polishing something
that's already clean, just making it look a little prettier.

And other times, you're working elbow deep in the sewer all
day – and, later that evening, it takes you about twelve
showers just to start feeling clean again!

But, in the long run, is any of it really *better* or *worse?*

I mean, dirt is still dirt, no matter where you find it.
So, in that sense, none of it is worth judging really.

And actually, most of the time, the harder work is actually
more enjoyable than the easy stuff.
Or, at least, brings a greater sense of achievement.
After all, any old clown can put a bit of polish on something
that is already clean.

But who out there is gonna be dedicated enough to actually get down amongst the dirt for real?

That takes a special kind of soul – no doubt about it.

And if you've got that level of heart in you - then that's when you've got every right to be proud of what you're doing!

(Even if it does take twelve showers to start feeling it!)

Call me an ambulance

Two more young idiots really testing my patience today.

Saturday afternoon gangsters; acting all tough, when you know they're both going home to mummy's cooking later tonight.

I noticed them earlier this morning too, when they must have walked past the cafe at least seven times, before actually deciding to come in.

But, as soon as they finally did sit down, it was like they were in competition to see who could act like the biggest asshole in here.
And, if that was the case, then the older of the two was clearly the winner.

I reckon he must have been late teens. Maybe even early twenties.
But, for the entertainment of his tubby little sidekick, he was acting like a damn twelve-year-old;
throwing peanuts across the café, and dripping tomato sauce all over the floors that I'd only just cleaned.

At one point, I even heard his little sidekick say
"Bruv – give it a rest now. This place is disgusting enough as it is!".

And, at this – the older guy had the nerve to reply;
"Yeah, tell me about it.

But, no surprise really.
You seen the guy they've got cleaning?
He looks like he don't even wash himself properly - so how's he ever
gonna get the hang of floors or tables instead!!"

Man, I tell you.
When I heard this little sonofabitch say that, it took all my self-restraint to resist going over there and knocking the teeth out of his smile!

But, to be fair, if I'd done that, then I'd only have to clean it all up again anyway.

And, besides, I love this job too much to risk it on an idiot like that.

So, in the end, I just put my head down,
pretending not to hear them.

And they kept up all their juvenile antics until around fifteen minutes later, when Maya (one of the new waitresses) came in to start her shift for the afternoon.

This is where the whole energy in the place shifted.

See, Maya is a young girl who has been working in here for just under a month now. But, with the self-assurance of someone twice her age, she's already well on her way to running the place!

And no surprise, really.

I mean, I heard she comes from a tough family– with two brothers who are nightclub doormen, and a father who was once a bare-knuckle boxer.

But, at the same time, this girl's also got the kind of face you could put on a magazine!
So, whenever she steps into the café, it's genuinely like a damn movie star has just arrived on set.

Anyway – she definitely had more than her usual affect here. Because, all of a sudden, these two idiots started playing everything so cool again; rolling a few cigarettes between them, with the older of the two making eyes at Maya every so often – clearly racking his brain for ways he could try to impress her.

Eventually, he even plucked up the courage to call her over to their table.

And from my little corner, I just watched on – to see what kind of game he would try to play.

"Hey. Excuse me!" he said.
"Yeah. . . Can I get, uh . . . two more cups of coffee please? Large – with two sugars each"

"Sure" Maya replied
"Anything else?"

"Well. Actually . . ." the little prick started grinning

"Yeah. Just one other thing.
Real quick . . .
You're gorgeous. Do you know that?
I mean, for real. I'm surprised I've not seen you around
before . . .
Where are you from?"

Then . . . he waited.

He waited because I guess he'd hoped for a blush.
Or a thank you.
Or, at the very least, a little smile in return.

But, instead, there was nothing.

Maya stared back at him. And the silence between the two
of them just sat there – right until it was getting awkward
for just about everyone else in the place too.

Then, cold as anything, Maya said
"Ok. Just two coffees then"
And wrote something on her little paper slip. (Probably
along the lines of *"Remember to spit in these guys drinks!"*)

Here, the guy frowned.
Shooting a quick glance with his buddy
as if to say *"what the hell just happened?"*

"What? You're not even gonna answer my question? He said

And once again, Maya didn't even bother to reply

"Come on. Don't be shy." He insisted "Where are you from?"

Maya sighed
"I'm not from here"

"Then . . . tell me"

"Somewhere else"

And with that, she turned her back on the two of them – heading back to the counter.

Now, at this point; any normal person would have gotten the message, and given up.

Clearly, whatever movie the guy had stolen this line from was never going to match up to the way things happen in real life.

And in fact, as much as I couldn't stand the two of them – even I was over here silently thinking to myself;
"Boy, just do yourself a favour and let it be. She's obviously not interested!"

But. of course,
this young guy thought he was a big man, right?
Casanova in a grey tracksuit!

So, when Maya eventually came back with the two cups of
coffee, (Having purposely left them waiting for as long as
possible) he again tried to engage with her

"Hey. Thanks a lot.
Much appreciated.
But, can I just check;
this cup is the large coffee right?"

"Yeah" said Maya

"With 2 sugars?

"That's what you asked for"

"Ok, cool.
And how much is it again?"

She told him the price

"Alright" said the young guy "So, if it's that much for just a
drink . . . how much would I have to pay in tips in order to
get your phone number too?"

Here, Maya took a step backwards.
Not out of fear – more like she was sizing the fella up.

"How much?" she said, with a tut
"Sweetheart – you couldn't afford it. Trust me.
And anyway, I don't go around with little boys like you!"

By now, place was completely silent.

Literally, it felt like the entire neighbourhood had stopped
to see how this was going to all play out. And, clearly, the
guy was really starting to twitch under all the pressure.

"Little boy?" he spat "Are you for real?"

"Yeah" Maya snapped back "You didn't hear me properly?
Ok, I'll try again, *little boy*.
Listen closely.
You got money to spend on a girl? Then go to the
whorehouse down the street.
If they let you in . . . maybe they'll have someone stupid
enough to give you the time of day.
But here? You better believe, I'm not playing games.
 Especially not with some ugly, dumb ass, pathetic boy
in a stupid dirty tracksuit. . . acting the prick, and thinking
he's slick.
It's really not my type.
You get me, *little boy*?"

With every word, the guy's face turned a darker shade of
purple.

He shot up out of his seat, crying;
"BITCH, I'LL SHOW YOU WHO'S A LITTLE BOY"

But, no sooner was he up – than he was on his way back
down again.

Maya threw the contents of two coffee cups directly in his
face,
and then landed a punch so hard on his nose you could hear
the crack echo around the entire café.

Immediately, his chubby friend leapt out of his seat.
(Not to fight . . . just to get out of Maya's range in case she
turned on him too)

And as he dashed to the doorway,
his buddy lay there on the floor in agony;
clutching his face, with coffee and blood spilling all around
him.

No-one else in the café made a move.
(I guess because the guy had irritated everyone so much at
this point, that they wouldn't have cared much even if she'd
killed him)

And, as for me – my first thought was pretty much just
*"Oh, great. On top of everything else, I've got to deal with this idiot
leaving blood stains on my floor too! "*

So, the only person who stepped in closer to him, was Maya.
And you could just tell, if this had been out on the streets,
she would have kicked the shit out of him for real.

But, instead, she just crouched down by his side, and grabbed him by the ear;

"Go on. Say something else to me, little boy!
Huh?
What's that?
Say something else to me!!
Call me a bitch again – and see what happens.
Because next time, I guarantee,
I'll break more than your nose.
You understand? "

The guy gave a pathetic little nod – and she stood up again. Crossing the floor back towards the counter, as if this was the most ordinary thing in the world.

"I'm . . . I'm bleeding!" The young fella whimpered "Someone, call me an ambulance!"

And, to be honest – this is the moment that made me fall just a little bit in love with Maya

Because, without missing a beat – from all the way over from behind the counter – she just replied
"Ok.

You're an ambulance!

Now . . . get the fuck out of here!"

Nothing lasts for very long

Good God. They say hell hath no fury like a woman
scorned! But clearly, whoever came up with that
must never have seen what a girl like Maya can do
when someone calls her a bitch!

And I love that she just went right back to work after that
too, as if nothing had happened.
(Didn't even offer to help me clean up the blood or the
coffee that she'd thrown; because, clearly, she saw it like her
work was already done.)

But to be fair, in a place like this
that's just how these things go.
Nothing ever lasts for very long!

You could drop dead right in the middle of the floor here
one morning;
and, by afternoon, they'd probably be serving drinks again,
with everything completely forgotten.

(Unless it was me who dropped down dead . . . in which
case, it would still get forgotten, but maybe just take a little
longer to get cleaned up properly!)

So it's funny to think that tonight, no-one in here is
bothered about what happened earlier.

And by tomorrow, the world will have just moved right
along.

And, even in a month or two's time; my guess is, Maya will
probably leave for a different job –
just like Jess, Will, Jon,
Izzy, Petra,
Remi, Sophia
and all the countless others
who only ever work here for such a short space of time too!

Yeah.
That much is guaranteed, isn't it!

A girl like that will never stay around here for long.

Because nothing ever stays around here for very long, really.

Only me.

It's just one day

Sometimes – you've just got to keep on keeping on.

Even when you're surround by all this hurt,
and all these hardships.

And living with all these memories.

And drowning in all this dirt.

You've just got to keep doing whatever you can to get by.

You tell yourself
It's just one day

It's just one day

It's just one day

And then
After about a thousand "Just one days"
You start to realise

Nah, man
It was never "just one day"
was it!

The stray dog

There's a stray dog that's been showing up around the Cafe for the last few days. And damn near every person that comes in here is talking about it

"Have you seen the dog?"

"Poor thing, looks so lonely"

"All skin and bones . . ."

"And those bald patches on its back . . ."

"Has anyone been feeding it?"

"Where do you think it's come from?

"It looks so sad"

"Has anyone called the authorities?"

"Surely it must have a family somewhere to look after it"

"If not . . . let me know. I'll give it a good home. I love dogs!"

Yeah.
The charity is endless when it comes to a stray like that.

And yet, all the while,

about three doors down from here,
there's a young homeless fella who I've noticed just recently
pitched up too.

He doesn't speak a word of English.
Doesn't have a thing in this world, except for a green
rucksack and a sleeping bag.
And he doesn't even beg for money . . . nor food . . . nor
shelter.
Nothing
Just sits there in the doorway, with his knees hugged in tight
to his chest; watching the world pass in front of him.

And do you know something?

With all these animal lovers going out of their minds with
worry about the damn dog . . . I've not heard a single person
mention him instead.

Not even once.

So . . . what?
You're telling me everyone's too busy looking at the dog
that no-one's noticed him?

They're not worried about where *he* comes from too?
Or what *he's* eating?
Or who's gonna look after *him*?
Or why *he* looks so sad?
Or what can be done to give *him* a good home too?

Man, how insensitive can these people be!

Trust me; if I ever see this dog for myself,
I'm just gonna tell it to go sit with that poor guy in the
doorway.

Then at least they'd both get a little company.
And maybe all of these insincere Samaritans around here
would actually start looking out for *both* of them together.

City of Angels

A lot of people don't believe in angels.

But me?
I think they're real;
it's just that we look for them in the wrong places.

Like, for example;
if angels genuinely do exist – do you really think they'd all
just be up there hanging out on a cloud somewhere; playing
silly harp music, and curling their hair?

That seems kind of callous, if anything,
given how much of a struggle this life can be.

And, honestly, if that is the truth, then tell those angels they
can stay the hell away from me!
Because trust me, the kind of angels that I believe in
wouldn't be up there in the skies.

Rather, they'd be down here in the dirt instead
probably disguised as the stray dog . . . or the guy in the
doorway . . . or Nanna. . . or Sarah. . . or Mad Leo . . . or
that old guy Vinny, who I never got to know.

These people are angels for real,
because they're the ones who see humanity for what it really
is – right?
Beyond all pretence.

And sure, if a white robed woman with wings and a halo walks into this café tonight, I guarantee everyone will be on their best behaviour.

But, is anyone gonna be just as friendly when it's an old down and out in the café instead – who just wants enough change to buy a pack of cigarettes?

I guess we'll wait and see.

All I know is, you can tell more about someone's soul by how they act in the dirtiest places, rather than in the cleanest.

So, if angels really do exist,
then I guarantee they'd be down here amongst the broken.
Not just watching for afar, while everything goes ahead and breaks some more.

Street Philosophy

Long before there were any schools or universities - every branch of philosophy developed first on the streets.

And even these days – in a place as downtrodden as this – you only have to listen to how people talk, and you realise that everyone's a philosopher to some extent. Whether they realize it or not.

I mean, scientists might talk about this Darwinian thing all the time in their safe little lecture halls.
But if you want to understand survival of the fittest for real – go speak to gang runners and guys on the street.

They'll tell you in no uncertain terms.
'It's a dirty game in this city. So, you've got two choices.
You either play . . . or you end up getting played,
You step . . . or you get stepped on
It's Kill or be killed.
That's just the way this world works."

But, then, ask someone else for another perspective, and, like any great university, you can always find something totally different.

For example, when you talk to the Drunks – you'll hear something closer to the Epicurean.

They say: *"Nah, man. it's not about trying to be the king of the jungle
out here.*
We're here for a good time — not a long time.
So don't worry about none of this other shit.
Just enjoy yourself, however you can!
*Because it's better to be out here drowning your sorrows . . . than letting
them drown you instead"*

Then, you've got office workers - who are more into Faith
over Science.
And these guys tell the drunks: "No. *that's not how it's supposed
to be either.*
Life can't just be one big party all the time!
We have to sacrifice now for reward later on!
*But, reast assured, if we just grind out a few more years slaving away
in this job . . . then maybe we'll have enough money saved up to really
make it to paradise."*

And then the taxi cab or bus drivers come along, like our
saints and martyrs — saying *"Hey, man - don't talk to us about
paradise! We gave up on all those dreams a long time ago! Because,
actually, all we have is now. And it's about helping others get to where
they need to be . . . even if that means going around in circles, never
getting anywhere for ourselves!"*

And then the rich folks are like our prosperity gospel
preachers — telling each other *"All these people are so desperately
wrong! The Kingdom of heaven is here. And all things are already ours
to indulge in anyway! It's just that, sadly, the good life is not for
everyone. We inherited this life through past good deeds. And, good
lord, we'll enjoy what we so rightly deserve!"*

And then, when a certain section of tramps or wasters hear the rich folks talking like that . . . they counter with a bit of atheism – saying; *"Seriously? The kingdom of heaven is here . . . huh? Well, then why the hell are we out here freezing our asses off and starving to death? You think that sounds like paradise? You think we deserve to have nothing, while you have everything? You think a God up in the sky would really choose to torture us like this?"*

See what I mean?

Damn near everyone is working on their own theories out here.

And at the end of the day – who's got it correct?

It could be all of them.

It could be none of them.

It could be a mixture.

I guess we'll find out one day.

Salvation

Eventually, we learn everything – or we stop asking questions.
It's as simple as that.

So, who knows what the future will bring?

*

Maybe in time, this neighbourhood will just keep getting dirtier and dirtier. (In spite of my efforts!)

And maybe tragic shit is inevitable in this life, no matter how hard we try to avoid it.

And maybe this world of ours really will go up in flames; just like the street preachers are always predicting.

But if cleaning can be an example for anything at all; it's that there's always a chance that things can be made better too – regardless of who caused this mess, or how it got here.

So, just put the work in.
That's all I can say.

Put the damn work in

And see what happens.

Then, one of these days, perhaps the tragedies of the past will be explained in the wisdom of the future.

And perhaps those black brick buildings will be made clean again.

And the Silver Spoon Café will get a repaint

And the drunks will all sober up.

And the addicts will get clean.

And all the lonely people will finally find their place to belong.

And the streets will be made safer

And poor Marco, wherever he is, will get a run of luck.

And Demani will sing again.

And Yuri will make it to heaven

And Leo will find the mind he lost.

And old Vinny will finally come back to sit here in his little window seat . . .

*

Literally, anything is possible.

And in that case, all I know is this;

In a world where every single one of us will inevitably lose
love, luck, and life. . .

The trick is
to never
lose
hope.

About the Author

George Bothamley is a London born Writer and Artist

Though predominately self-educated, he developed as a writer due to a particular love of reading classic literature. And, alongside a prolific output of Poetry, Fine art, and Philosophical essays – he has also published four books to date, including;

The Diary of and Old Dunk (Fiction – 2017)
Poor Guy (Short Story – 2018)
Stories of Sages and Sibyls (Fable collection - 2020)
Photo Meditations (Poetry/Prose – 2022)

For more books and updates on new releases coming soon, please visit

www.georgebothamley.co.uk